One

by Eric Devine

ONE IN TEN

First edition. April 21, 2020.

Written by Eric Devine.

For everyone bound to addiction:
fight, before even that is taken away
from you

1

Here's the secret no one tells you: drugs are fun. I know a lot of addicts and I can't think of one who started using because they wanted to feel bad. It's the opposite. We all know what could go wrong, both long and short term. But that's a gamble, that's life. Therefore, it's worth rolling the dice, because snake eyes are a potential, but so are those double six boxcars. The risk is worth the reward of escaping from this world. Every. Single. Time.

No one really tells you about rehab, either. Not early on, not when you're partying and able to get through the next day clean. Then, you know of people who had to go, and everyone laughs about them, but secretly we don't want to become them. So, sometimes we go on little clean stints, mini-sobriety days or weeks, if we can manage them. We still use, but only enough so we don't lose our minds. So we don't have a seizure and then have no choice about rehab.

Here's another secret, maybe the last one, maybe the biggest of all. Being clean is hell. This is my third time. Who knew by seventeen I'd go through three centers? Certainly not my parents. I'm sure they imagined their boy growing up to be a doctor or lawyer or any of those other cliché things. No one wants a junkie. But that's what I am, who I grew up to be. That's why being clean is hell. It's not who I am, but who I will forever be.

Yet, this clean has to be permanent. The third time has to be the charm. If not, the government owns me.

However, with my relatives pulling into the driveway and parking on the side lawn, all here to celebrate the fact that I'm done, really done, I'm not sure what to feel. I should be thrilled for the support. Excited for the change. But if I'm being honest, I'm scared out of my mind. What am I going to do now? As in right now. As in a day from now. As in, after. I know drugs. I know being high. My way of getting through all my rehabs, including this last one, was the idea that there's an escape hatch to this real world: I could always use again.

The knock on my door startles me away from the window. Mom walks in, sees me jump. "Did I scare you?" she asks, but isn't interested in a response. This victory is her victory, too.

"I just wasn't expecting *everyone*. Is that Uncle Theo's car?"

She moves to the window, but places a hand on my elbow, as if to keep me tethered. As if I'm a balloon.

"It is. Don't know how he keeps it running." She turns back and looks me over. Her smile slips. "You feeling all right? You're pale." Mom touches my forehead with the back of her hand. It's sad how she thinks she can somehow still take care of me, can understand what's actually wrong.

"There's just a lot of people, all that attention," I say.

"They love you. There's nothing to be afraid of." She holds me at arm's length. "You're a success story. Remember, your cousin, Gene, he still can't get clean. And that Bobby you were friends with, he just entered the government program. They haven't heard from him."

I hate how she lets this hang, instead of saying what she thinks: *I'll be like Bobby if I start using again*. I'd just begun the last facility when they passed the law. Private insurance is no longer allowed to pay for rehab. The government is sick of the "waste." It's not clear if they mean us or the money spent. Regardless, we thought this was great news. Not having to break our parents' banks any more was such a relief. You'd be surprised at the amount of guilt we hold. Then one of the counselors explained how the program works. When he finished telling us, it was as if he'd described how each of us would die, and somehow, we had to find the will to get clean. We watched as they transitioned the center over while we were getting sober. The writing was on the wall: *This is your last chance*.

"Hey, there you are," Dad says from the door. I don't know if he means Mom or me, but the way his eyes don't meet mine helps me with the answer. "The pizza guy's here. Which card am I supposed to use?" He lowers his voice when he asks, and I feel the weight of Mom's answer hang from me.

"The red one. There's nothing in the account until I get paid Friday."

Dad nods, looks like he's about to say something, but then someone's calling for him from the other room, probably one of his cousins letting him know about the pizza guy at the door. The pizza guy that Dad will pay with a credit card, because each one of my rehabs cost more than any vacation they could have ever dreamed of. And if they did, those dreams went up in smoke.

Mom pats my hand. "We're fine. You're fine. Everything's going to be all right. Take a minute if you need, but then come on out. They're here for you."

This sounds more like a threat than support, but I nod and say, "Okay," and then she's gone. I look out my window again. It's a gorgeous spring day, almost summer. I haven't felt a day like this in years. I've been too absorbed in my drug-bubble world. The breeze blows through the window, bringing with it the scent of flowers and grass. It's too real. I shut my window, take a breath, and walk out of my room to face my family.

"There he is!" someone yells. I look around the room and try to identify who spoke, but it's useless, they're all moving toward me now, no regard for personal space. Aunts grab my cheeks, uncles clap my shoulders, cousins say I don't look so bad for a junkie. This is the third time we've done this, and their enthusiasm surprises me. Yet, it's not as if they don't know what I know. This time their support has to stick.

I am a junkie. I'm in love with heroin. I do look better than most, but it's taken me months to get looking this good again, to sleep again, to regain an appetite. This façade is going to be impossible to keep up.

They manage to sit me in a chair directly in front of a table of presents. I can't remember the last time I had a party with gifts. Was it seventh grade? I wasn't using then. Drinking, yeah. After. After is a long stretch of blackouts and missing time.

"Open! Open!" They yell at me like I'm eight years old, again, and I oblige. It's weird, I want to open these gifts, even though I can sense from the size and shape, most will be clothing and gift cards.

And they are. But as I open each one, I take my time. I say thank you. I tally up, in my head, what each pair of ugly shorts and each collared shirt might net me when I return them. I try and fail to restrain myself from equating that money into drugs. There's a long pause and I look over the table to see if I missed a bag.

My uncle Theo approaches, all beard and beady eyes. He stares for a moment too long and I look away. Before I went to rehab, I said some awful things to him. Called him washed up. Told him he'd wasted his life, that he could have been someone. That he no longer has talent.

He used to write freelance scripts. He's not connected to Hollywood, but some of his work has been produced, so he tells us. Theo also used. Coke was his thing, but it ruined him as well. I know now that when I was yelling at him, I was yelling at myself, or some version of who I was. Doesn't matter that I was coming down, and miserable, I still said those things, more than once. Yet, here is my uncle, awkwardly standing before me with a thick gift, his eyes boring into me.

"What's this?" I ask, taking the package from him.

"You'll see," he whispers. Around his head, phones come out. They're recording this. Shit.

I pull out a journal. Not some new, moleskine one, but an old, slightly warped composition notebook.

I look at Theo. "What?"

He laughs and his beard parts to reveal his teeth. He's furiously happy, and in a second his arms are around me. Theo squeezes for a moment and then we separate. "It's my journal. The one from when I finally got clean."

I open the pages in front of me and Theo tenses. He's talked about this journal so many times I've wondered if it was real. How does a junkie keep track of anything? I guess we do whatever's necessary for the things that matter most, like our drugs.

"Remember," he says, "It's like the *Basketball Diaries*."

I remember. I even watched the movie version of the memoir a couple of years ago. That guy got it right, but it didn't inspire me to quit, just made me realize I'd have great material for a book someday.

"I haven't read it in a while," Theo says, "so I apologize if it's a mess in spots, but trust me, it will help you."

There's no way he can know this. I've been told the same line by countless therapists and psychiatrists. Nothing has worked. But it would be good if this did. The government's plans for me are much worse.

"Thanks," I say. "I appreciate this."

"We can talk as you go. Just keep me in the loop. Okay?"

His face is inches from my own; it's all I can see. And I know before I speak that I never want this to be my reflection. "Absolutely."

A tear cascades into Theo's beard. "Kenny, it will work this time."

There's applause and tears and my family thanks Theo and then someone says, "Let's eat!" and the room moves toward the table and the pizza and the side dishes that were brought.

I sit, unable to comprehend. Or capable, just unwilling. Mom and Dad come over.

"You okay?" Mom asks.

"Yeah, just, wow. He's talked about it, but here it is." I hold up the beaten down journal.

"I've read some of it," Dad says. "I agree with him. It could help you, and so many others. Why he hasn't tried to get it published is beyond me."

It isn't beyond me. I've had to keep journals every place I've been. If anyone ever read them, or worse, published them? Nope. Just, nope.

"Come on, let's eat," Mom says. She slaps my thigh to get me to stand. One day home and the typical routines are falling into place.

I stand and it's too much. Something about the smell of the pizza or the body heat of the room makes me want air. "I'll be right back," I say, holding up the journal as reason for leaving, and go to my room. I close the door behind me and the space is as stifling as the rest of the house.

I don't want air.

If I really wanted air I would have walked outside, onto the front stoop or the back patio. I wait to see if they follow me. There are no footsteps, just laughter and merriment beyond the door. And why wouldn't there be? *Kenny's home, and he looks so good, and Theo's words will save him.* My parents should have paid more attention to the instructions they were given. I shouldn't be alone like this. But there's pizza and family and happiness, something they haven't had in quite some time. It's euphoric, something I understand perfectly.

I rifle through my desk drawer. I noticed yesterday that they'd cleaned it, but they didn't remove everything. This is not exactly a clean slate. You think they would have learned. Or, maybe I was just good at covering my tracks. Either way, the flat-head screwdriver is still in the bottom drawer. What do they think I use it for?

I take it and go to my closet. The baseboard appears the same, but there's only one way to find out. My heart begins to trot inside my chest. I can hear them talking about me just beyond the door, and I'm careful to keep an ear trained for anyone calling. I bend over and my face feels like a mask as blood pounds in my ears. My chest is tight and my eyes bulge. I can make out the Velcro from here. I get on one knee and my heart is thrumming.

The screwdriver slides in neatly and I pry. The section pops loose and reveals one of my stash spots. Apparently, one they never found, because either I'm hallucinating, or there's a baggie still inside.

I rub a hand over my face. It slides over the tacky sweat that has blossomed. The fear I felt is gone, and only in this moment I realize how alive I feel. Not uncertain, not insecure, not bumbling around hospital hallways and cafeterias and therapy rooms. This is me, kneeling before a year-old bag of heroin, happier than Theo was to hand me a future. I'm pleased with my past self. I know him so much better.

My hand goes into the hole. Really, it's as if my hand is acting on its own volition. I'm merely watching it, and smiling at it, and cheering for it. Like this is some twisted claw game at an arcade.

It returns, and does not let me down. The bag sits in my palm, the exterior smooth and white, some sort of devil image stamped on the front staring up at me. It had a name, but I can't recall it. My brain is swimming, pleading, moaning. Thought is almost impossible.

"Where's Kenny?" The voice is clear and well outside my room, but I know where it will lead, and I cannot have that.

I reconnect the Velcro and then slide the baggie into my pocket. It burns, a reminder of possibility, of that escape. But not now. I can't risk it now. I've been clean long enough to recognize that. My heart is still running double-time and I sit on the edge of my bed and hold my breath, try to slow it all down.

The door opens and Mom comes through. "You okay?"

"Yeah, yeah, just a little overwhelmed. I needed a second."

She sits next to me and I tilt toward her. "I understand, but don't run off like that. I got a little nervous."

I don't look her in the eye. Can't. "That makes sense. Theo's gift—I don't know, the implication of this not working—I'm scared." The honesty shocks me. The fact that I have heroin in my pocket does not negate the fact that I want to be clean. I do.

She rubs my back. "Be in the here and now. It's all that you need to focus on. Right now, your family is here. Right now, you are clean. Right now, I am sitting next to you, on your bed, in your room. How long's it been since we've been able to do this?" Her voice drops with the last question.

I don't want her to cry, and I know she's about to. She should be happy. I can hold my shit together for a little while longer. Maybe I can even just taste the heroin and then flush it. One parting gift. This thought gives me strength. I take Mom's hand. "Come on. The here and now says I'm starving."

She laughs harder than she should and we stand. When we walk into the living room, I see the anxiety on faces slip away. I capitalize on that. "Is there any pepperoni left?"

This brings forth a series of scampering, and in a second I have a plate with two enormous pieces of pepperoni pizza on it. I chomp into the first and the room relaxes. I smile around the dough and look over the room. Dad and Theo are standing together. They have the same look on their faces. They know. Neither is eating. Both stare. Sweat breaks out along my back.

"Huh, it does look like a duck," Theo says.

"Told you," Dad replies.

I turn and see the cheap painting that they are looking at. One they must have purchased while I was away. Something, I bet, to cover the holes in the wall behind that frame.

2

The party ends with my relatives taking just enough leftovers so that we still have food for tomorrow. Dad walks Theo out. He squeezed my arm before he went, but fortunately didn't offer any more advice. I don't think I could have handled it. About all I can handle right now is the sensation of this bag in my pocket. I have to do something with it. This is not a choice. This is addiction in the real-world, not some stupid treatment center where there aren't any drugs.

Mom's in the kitchen, tidying up. The sound of the Tupperware lids snapping into place is comforting. I worked in the kitchen at my second treatment center. We packaged a lot of leftovers, and I scrubbed a lot of Tupperware, but I loved that place. It was the cleanest, with the best-looking staff. Strange details like that matter. I was willing to do anything for this one, smoking hot counselor, Hannah. I was fifteen and she was probably in her twenties, and holy hell, every time she smiled, I melted a little. It was like the tiniest bump of H, but it did the trick.

Only for so long, though. The memory of her faded not long after I got home and I needed real drugs, not smiles.

"Do you need any help?" I ask, while holding onto the wall leading into the kitchen. I want her to say no, but I'm trying not to live like the asshole I usually am. Or maybe I'm stalling, trying to stifle the baggie's voice.

Mom looks around the room. "No, I've got it." She looks at me. "Did you have fun?"

I wouldn't call that gathering *fun*, but I say, "Absolutely. So much better than what I was doing this time last week."

Instead of laughing at my joke her face loses its levity. She looks downright sad for a moment, before saying, "Right. But you're here now."

It sounds like she's convincing herself of this fact.

"Yeah. Sorry, I didn't mean to upset you."

Her head snaps. "No, I'm not upset. Not at all." She forces a wide, fake smile, and as much as I know what's going on with her, I don't really know. I've been away and they've been here, struggling, for sure. Financially, emotionally, and in ways I can't comprehend. That's what therapy gets you to consider, but then baggies and potential scores and old connections help you forget.

The front door opens and Dad comes in, laughing. "Man, Theo is in a great mood."

Mom raises her eyebrows at me, and we both turn to greet him.

"Seriously, he was just cracking jokes and telling me about this project he's working on."

"You believe him?" I ask.

Dad grabs a carrot from the wings' container. He bites down. "What do you mean?"

How does he not understand? "Do you think he's really working on something? Not just blowing smoke?"

My parents look at one another. It's one of those unspoken communication moments. Then Dad nods. He looks back at me. "Kenny, Theo is actually doing well. He's writing for Netflix."

"What?" I'm genuinely confused. Theo's always been evasive about his work, so how can Dad *know* this?

"I'll show you. His name's on the credits for a few of the shows. It's legit."

"So why's he still driving that crappy car of his?"

Another moment of silence, another silent communication between them. Then Mom answers. "He's still paying off his rehab bill."

That hurts. But it also makes sense. Theo didn't go away until he was older. He was an adult, which means he got to foot the bill. It's not as if Dad's parents would have helped anyway. They have that mantra of *You made your bed, now you're going to lie in it*. Always seemed harsh to me.

"Well," I say, and don't have anything more.

Dad clasps my shoulder. "Hey, the best thing is he's left you with that gift, his journal. You won't question the legitimacy of what's there, trust me."

"Don, don't push," Mom says.

Dad squeezes my shoulder a bit tighter. "I'm not, just offering some advice."

His words echo through me, as do the memories of our meetings with therapists, pre-release. They have all these rules, which makes it feel like they're trying to bring the facility into the real world. But we all follow them, like New Year's resolutions, and just as quickly, we fall back into what we know. Dad's on script, and so is Mom, and so I know my line.

"It's all right. I actually want to chill for a bit. Maybe I'll read some of the journal."

Behind me, Mom says, "That's your choice, honey."

Dad nods. I'm in one hell of a supportive sandwich, and yet it feels stifling.

"Thanks," I say, and take a step toward my room. "And don't let me forget to call Henry later. I now he's got meetings lined up." He's my sponsor and is probably itching to hear what's what.

"You got it," they say, in unison, and then they laugh, which makes me smile, because if they can still do that together, all is not lost. So maybe, neither am I.

I grab Theo's journal and settle onto my bed. Once there, my leg burns. It's like having a toothache. You literally can't think of anything else besides the pain. Until you figure something out, like pinching yourself, or stabbing your arm with a pencil, repeatedly. It was the stupidest thing for me not to tell anyone about the stash. This is my fault. Yeah, I wasn't one-hundred percent certain that there were drugs there, but it would have been so much better if my parents had found this bag, searching on a maybe, than me, practically willing it into existence.

It's like I've forgotten everything I've been through, all that I've learned at the treatment centers I've been in. Somehow, I've seemed to misplace all my logic, because do I really want to lose it all to the government? Don't I want to be clean?

I grab a pillow and jam it over my face and scream. I bite the pillow and scream some more and the anger outweighs the tears I know are coming next, followed by my self-hatred, which gives me all the excuse I need to use again.

Air. I inhale deeply, fill my belly and count to five. I repeat the process until I'm no longer panicking. At the edge of my dresser sits my uncle's journal. Beyond it is my closet. This feels like a path, and I'd better start on it straight, because I've already started to detour.

I move as fast as I can, so I don't have to think. My hand's in my pocket as I reach the closet, but I've forgotten the screwdriver, and now the baggie sits in my hand, winking at me. I kneel down and dig my fingertips in and yank.

The Velcro budges, but not much. The baggie feels like it's crawling up my arm, guided by GPS, marking the way to the crook, to my veins, which are healthy again, bulging blue. I put my shoulder into it this time and don't care that my knuckles are scraping. I push down as hard as I can and the board gives way. The hole from which the baggie came is open. This is like some paranormal movie and I have to return the demon to the other world, and so I do. I play the hero. I toss the baggie in, snap the board back in place, and then hear the scream from the other side, the pain of death.

Except there is no voice and there is no death, and I could be the antihero at any moment. For now, I'm safe, and a certain calmness washes over me. I've won the battle. But I've fought so many that this one feels hollow.

I stand, grab my uncle's journal and take it back to my bed. I breathe, and then before I can think another thought about drugs, I open the damn thing and read.

On the inside cover, Theo's written: *The rules are at the end. A list. To understand them, though, you must start at the beginning.*

"Okay, Yoda," I say, and turn to the back. Sure enough, Theo's five rules are scrawled.

1. Honesty, at all times, with yourself and others.
2. A mind works best when it's open, so drop your judgment and your preconceptions.
3. You are your surroundings, so be sure that who and what are around you reflect what you want to see in yourself.
4. Avoid temptations of all varieties, because if there is no spark, you cannot have fire.
5. Believe in something greater than yourself. This doesn't have to be God, but it does have to possess the same power as one.

None of these are new ideas. I've heard some variation of these ever since I began using, or really since my parents tried to stop me from using. How is this supposed to save me? I don't even know how to do half of this, and I'll bet not even sober people do.

I set the journal down and look out my window. Night has fallen and the moon is shrouded in clouds. "Fuck you, Theo," I say. "Like you have a clue."

There's a knock at the door and then Mom's walking in. "Are you okay?" Her eyes are all over me, looking, searching, praying.

"Yeah, I just started Theo's journal. It's got me thinking."

"Oh." It's obvious that she's not sure how to proceed. Should she leave me with these thoughts or not? She holds out her phone. "Well, this may be perfect timing, then. Henry called."

It's like she's pointing a gun at me. I'd rather her pull the trigger than make me talk to him. Not right now. He'll hear in my voice that I'm desperate, that my mind's not like a parachute, and that the only belief I have is that this will not end well.

"Uh, great. That is like *perfect timing*," I say and reach for the phone.

Mom holds onto it for a second and cannot contain her smile. "Let me know when you're done." She closes the door and I put the phone up to my ear.

"Henry, hey, it's Kenny."

"It sure as hell better be you. I don't want to know if you have anyone else in the room with you." He laughs at his own joke and I chuckle along because it's polite. There's no one else in my life, male or female. Once I started using, drugs were all that mattered. I know I've hooked up with people, but I can barely remember what happened. And in rehab you can't touch anyone but yourself. And even then, you feel so guilty all the time, it barely rises.

"On a scale of one to ten, how much do you want to use right now?" Henry, he cuts to the damn chase.

I know I'm at like an eight, but if I say that, he'll have my parents sleeping in my room. "I won't lie, like a five."

"Bullshit. I talked to your mother. You've been pacing the house, you had a party, your uncle left you some words of wisdom. You're crawling out of your damn skin."

It sucks to be this transparent. Or obvious. Or a stupid stereotype. "All right, like an eight."

"Now that sounds about right. There's an NA meeting in a half hour at the Presbyterian church in town. You're going."

"But I'm so damn tired. Let me sleep the itch away."

"Yeah, because that works. Get your ass outta bed. Your dad probably has his keys in his hand already." There's a pause and in it I close my eyes and am thankful. "Got it?"

"I do. Thanks, Henry."

"Any time, Kenny. Work the steps."

I hang up. "Screw the steps," I mutter. I'm not sure if I mean this, but I've yet to find someone who has managed to get clean from following those twelve mantras. Yet, who am I to talk?

I take Henry's advice and get out of bed. Dad is in the hallway when I open my door. "You ready?" he says and holds up his keys as if to punctuate his question.

I pat myself down, out of habit, but I have no wallet or money or phone or drugs—at least not on me. "Yeah."

We walk out to the car and Dad pulls out of the driveway. I was in the backseat for the ride home, and that was a trip, because it had been so long since I'd been in a car, outside, and free. Now, in the passenger seat, I lower the window a crack and feel the air on my face.

"You feeling all right?" Dad asks.

"Better than I have in a while. It's the little things, like car rides and open windows. You forget about them."

He's quiet, probably wondering what else I've forgotten. The list could go on and on. We pull up to the church and a few people stand outside, smoking cigarettes, a sure sign we're in the right spot. "All right, so I'll see you in like an hour or so?" I ask.

Dad reaches into the back and pulls a plastic bag onto his lap. "Actually, you can call when you're done. That is if you still remember our numbers."

He hands me a Trac phone, which is this shitty Android, but it's a smart-phone, so I can't complain much. I tap the contacts. There are none. This is perfect, because, yes, I remember my parents' numbers, but none of my friends/dealers', whoever they were to me.

I dial and a moment later Dad's phone rings. He smiles.

"Put me in your contacts in case you want to text," I say.

"I will, Kenny," he says, but makes no move toward his phone. He looks me over and I know what he's going to say before he says it. "I'm proud of you. You did the work, inside, so let's continue it, outside."

Because it's that easy. The problem with addiction is that it's not compartmentalized. You can't fix one area, you have to fix them all, and I'm not sure anyone has figured out how to treat the entire person and their surroundings, and their past, and their habits, and every little trigger that becomes an excuse. But I say, "Couldn't agree more. Thanks, Dad." I tuck my new phone away and get out of the car, cross the street, and join the group outside the church.

There are no signs, so I ask a guy in his twenties who's smoked his cigarette down to the filter, "This NA?"

"Better be." He smiles. "If not, we're about to learn about Jesus or some shit."

I laugh and it feels good. The guy laughs back and nods toward the stairs. We descend for the meeting or for Jesus or for something else altogether.

3

There's a dozen of us, mostly young guys, but a few who are older, and two women, both just older than me. I'm not attracted to anyone particularly, but being around a group of people who remind me of all the kids I ran with gives me a rush. We shift around in our seats, as the moderator, an older, black, bald man, stands by the coffee pot and stale cookies. I've been to countless meetings like this, and I expect nothing to be different about this one. We'll talk about what we've done, what we want to do, and then I'll leave with an enormous urge to use.

"Ok, everyone, I think it's time to begin." The moderator sits in one of the empty chairs but eyes the door as if he's expecting someone else, and based on the handful of remaining chairs, he might be.

"My name is Marcus and I am an addict. I've been clean for ten years and twenty-four days. Heroin was my drug of choice." He looks to his right and one of the girls stops biting her nails so she can speak.

"My name's Jennifer and I'm an addict. I've been sober for nine months and three days. I also used H, but I'd settle for some damn good Oxy."

This pulls a laugh from the group, but not Marcus. He shakes his head. "Let's focus for now on your success. We'll help you with your cravings. Thank you, Jennifer."

Everyone introduces themselves and it's all the same; we're all addicted to heroin. Which, from what I've heard from other groups, both inside and out, is a change. There used to be Meth heads and Cocaine worshippers in groups, but they've all either switched to Heroin or stopped going to rehab.

Now it's my turn, and even though I know no one in this room is going to judge me, my heart hammers. I'm the youngest one here, and I know that doesn't matter because I've been using as long as some of the older members. Yet, it just feels different. As if my "kid" problems aren't enough evidence to make a case that I am truly an addict.

"Hi, I'm Kenny and I'm an addict. I've been sober for three months and one day, but that's only because I got out of rehab yesterday. I, too, am addicted to heroin."

There's a round of applause, as there always is for someone who's fresh out. But then, instead of moving on to the guy to my right, Marcus pins me with his eyes. "Kenny, is it okay if I ask how old you are?"

I sit up a little straighter and look to the remaining three people to my right. They understand, and one after the other spit out their names, length of sobriety, and heroin as their drug. Then it's right back to me.

"Well, I'm seventeen, but I started using around thirteen."

There's a gasp from some and murmurs from others, which I've experienced before. Not in the teen programs, obviously, but with the adults who are always like *Where were your parents?*

Marcus leans back. "Kenny, if you don't mind, let's start with you. What's your addiction story? How does a thirteen-year-old become an addict?"

My guess is that Marcus knows exactly how, but this is an easy way for him to burn some time and show the "old timers" who's creeping on their territory. Regardless, I give him the bulleted points.

"I had to get my wisdom teeth pulled because they were impacted—you know, coming in sideways—and so the doc prescribed Oxy for the pain. When I popped that first one, I felt the rush for the first time, and I was like, whatever this is, I want more. Then I learned how to crush and snort them, and then I ran out. My parents convinced the doc to give me more, but he was all, *Careful he doesn't get addicted.* Too late for that. After that script ran out, I don't know, it just became my thing to find people who had pills or connections. It's easier to do than most people think. Then I stole money from my parents and also stole from stores for the money, which I got arrested for, which is how my parents found out I was using. They made me see a doctor, which did no good because I lied about it all, blamed it on my new friends." I pause, look around the circle. "I didn't have any friends at that point. I had kids I used with." Some people smile, others nod, but Marcus looks at me likes he wants me to continue.

"So, yeah, then one day when I was in eighth grade, this guy I'd been scoring pills from was like, *You know, heroin is like the same thing, and cheaper. You want to try it out?* I was scared as hell. I'd never seen heroin before and I was all like fuck that. But then it's all I could think about, and sure enough, the next day I went back and the guy gave me my first bag. I snorted it, and after I came down realized this was exactly what I needed."

"And then?" Marcus says, and I realize I'm staring at the floor. It sounds fun as a story, but when I realize it's my life, it's embarrassing.

"And then I was using all the time, skipping school, all that. But the year ended. I graduated from eighth grade and graduated to needles. It's also easy to find someone with those, if you ask around. I started freshman year in a treatment facility, and I've basically earned a GED while in and out of centers, since. I've been to school for like twenty days or something over the last four years."

It's quiet when I finish telling my story. The chairs creak as the other members shift in their seats. The stale coffee wafts over me, and suddenly the heat is too much and I want the breeze from the car again. Or maybe I want that bag.

"How many kids at your school were using?" Jennifer asks.

"Hard drugs or just partying?"

"Please, I'm not even talking about pot and drinking."

Members laugh at this because it's true. I've seen kids function as pot heads, but no one functions as an addict.

"I don't know, a handful. We mostly connected with the high school kids."

"And how many of those older kids were there?" Marcus asks.

I'm not sure why they're so interested in this, but whatever. "A few dozen. You'd be surprised. Heroin is popular. Period. Look at us."

There are nods of agreement, but Marcus looks at me in that way again. "I'm sorry if you feel like I'm picking on you, Kenny. I'm just curious, because back in my day, it was just inner-city folk using H, and now, look at us—like you said—we're in the middle of suburbia, white folks everywhere, and all their kids are using. And with the new synthetics creeping in—"

"That's why the government's doing what it's doing," one of the older guys says, cutting off Marcus, who doesn't seem to mind. "They know they have to do something, because they can't allow the 'good people' to get used up."

"What do you mean by that? The *good people*?" the other woman asks.

"You heard Marcus," the older guy answers. "Used to be an inner-city thing. And what did they do to addicts? Arrested them. Now that it's spread out here, what do they do? Hand out Narcan. And since that's only a Band-

Aid, which is now falling off because of the sheer volume and the synthetics, they're going deep, making some real changes."

Marcus holds up his hand. "I don't want this to turn into a forum about the new policy. We can't change that. We should be focusing on ourselves and facing our personal addiction one day at a time."

The older guy who was talking just shakes his head. The younger guys look confused and the women are staring straight ahead. I get Marcus's point. One day at a time. Give yourself over to a higher power. Accept the things you cannot change. I *know* all this, but guess what? I still want to go home and use, and I don't know if this group or any therapist is going to change that. So I'm going to learn about my options. I raise my hand.

Marcus's eyebrows lift. "Kenny?"

"Let's just say, hypothetically speaking, that I have a bag at home."

This gets people's attention. Some literally snap at the words.

"Kenny, do you really have a bag?" Marcus asks.

"Let me finish," I say. "If I do, and I use, and then I do like I always do and just keep using until I'm completely strung out, what's going to happen to me? I have an idea, but I don't know what's true and what's rumor."

"Kenny, I already said that I don't want this to be a forum—"

"I hear you, but you're not listening to me. I'm just out of recovery, and I want to use again. You know my parents are going to bring me here and I'm going to try to work the steps and stay clean, but if I fail—" I look around the room. "If any of us fail, what is next? I'd really like to know the truth."

Marcus runs his palms along his legs and sits back. He looks around the circle and sees what I see, a bunch of people who are as genuinely interested as I am. Why wouldn't they be? It's their life and our stupid choices or addictions or terrible pasts that got us here. We should know which direction we should be more afraid of, the drugs or the program.

"Fine," Marcus says, "we'll spend some time talking about treatment, but you answer me one question, Kenny."

"Okay."

"Do you have a bag at home?"

This is a coin toss. If I say yes, he might throw me out of the meeting, or worse, tell my dad when he shows. If I say no, and he sees through the lie and clams up about what he knows, and I'll be left with my GED skills to figure out the intricacies of the program on my own.

"Yes," I say.

The room erupts with suggestions, all about flushing it or handing it over to my parents or the cops. I nod, knowing I'll do none of these.

Marcus looks at me. "You hear this. The choice is yours. Make the right one, because I don't think you're going to enjoy what I'm about to tell you."

The room goes quiet again. This group wants the truth. There's so much misinformation about what's going on, both inside centers and out, that even though I've been told, I'm not sure what to believe. But people who run these meetings, guys like Marcus who've been sober forever, they always know the truth, because for them, it's the thing that keeps them clean. Truth is power, and drugs are the ultimate power trip, making us feel invincible, if only for a little while. So I'm not surprised when these guys trade drugs for authority.

"The principle is that since we cost so damn much to rehabilitate because we keep using again and again, that we as patients must have a greater stake in the game. Also, since only people with good insurance or parents who can foot the bill for the nicer centers have the greatest success rate, that playing field needed to be leveled. Therefore, insurance no longer pays. Private individuals no longer pay. The rehab facilities are now government entities."

Everyone is hanging onto Marcus's every word. I know I've heard this, but I've ignored it. Other kids who came into treatment said the same, but they also said there's nowhere to go online to get more info. It's like no one's allowed to talk or write about it. Maybe that's true. This is the government.

"However, even though the government runs them, the primary 'employees' are you, the patients."

Now there's confusion and a lot of grumbling about what the hell he's talking about.

Marcus holds up a hand and we go quiet. "They're calling it One in Ten. Once you are through detox, not only are you going to have to work through your rehabilitation, you will also be responsible for seeing nine other people through theirs."

One of the guys laughs. "You're kidding. I can barely hold my own shit together, and they expect me to get nine others to figure it out?"

Marcus doesn't laugh along. His face draws serious. "That's the point. From what I hear they don't really care if you actually succeed. You don't leave until you hit your number."

"So, we're more like prisoners," Jennifer says.

"And the doctors are the wardens," the other woman says.

"Exactly," Marcus says. "They've successfully removed you and your crimes and your drain on the economy from the general population. You'll be a little bubble of addicts, and if you can't figure it out, that's all you'll ever be."

"How can't this be against the law?" one of the guys asks.

"Executive order," the older guy who brought this up, answers.

Marcus nods at him. "The ACLU tried to fight it and lost. There are other lawsuits, sure, but they'll lose, too. There's money in this. There's a promise being kept by our Commander in Chief. There are voters who agree with and believe in this."

"Holy shit," someone says, not angry, but as if he's deflating.

I have too many questions to sort through to even be able to ask any. My thoughts begin and are overtaken by others before I can finish. But I draw back to one point: this sounds like prison, but it's free. If I relapse, this is all on me. My parents won't have to worry. Maybe it's a dumb silver lining, but it's there, in front of me, just like that bag will be when I get home. As much as I don't want to be locked away, I also don't want to be a slave to a drug anymore. And Marcus seems like one of those doom and gloom kind of guys, who makes everything out to be the worst thing ever, when really, it's like everything else: shitty, but not the apocalypse.

"What's the success rate?" one of the younger guys asks, and I see a certain glint in his eye. I bet he's thinking what I am—safety net.

"It's too early to have hard numbers, but estimates from the first nine months suggest that ten percent will succeed in three months, another thirty percent in six months, and another twenty five percent in a year. There are no stats on recidivism."

"What about the other thirty five percent?" I ask.

Marcus gives me a cold look. "They're still inside."

4

The conversation at group never returns to our recovery. We all pepper Marcus with questions, and he does his best to answer, but while he's got the nuts and bolts, there are some holes in his knowledge. The buzz from my phone makes me jump, but I'm grateful for the text from Dad: *I'm outside. Find me when you're done.*

I pretend like I'm getting a bottle of water from the table and then slip out of the meeting. Dad's car is across the street.

"How was it?" he asks, while I buckle up.

"Not bad. Kind of the usual, but that's okay because it was a good group, a lot of younger people."

Dad pulls away and offers a slight nod. He's never been good at conversations about addiction. It's just not something he understands. "So, you want to go back there tomorrow? Because there are other meetings."

"No, I'll stay with them. I think it's a good fit," I say.

He looks at me and smiles like he's put that last puzzle piece in place.

We get home and Mom has the same questions as Dad, and acts equally pleased when I tell her that everything went so well. I've had some really bad group experiences, so I know how much this first, good meeting means to them.

"I'm going to shower and then go to bed. I'm exhausted."

"Okay," Mom says, and then kisses my cheek.

I turn away but not before I see their hands find each other's.

The shower feels amazing and I linger under the heat, letting it pour across the base of my neck. I'm trying to drown out the idea of having a bag in the house, but the water only turns down the volume. It can't mute it.

I get out, towel off, and dress, then remember I have to call Henry. Not because I want to, but because I understand protocol.

"How was it?" he asks. No greeting, just launches into it.

"Not bad, but we got talking about the new program."

"Sweet, Jesus! That wasn't the goal."

"Like I can control a meeting. But, anyway, is it really that bad? Because the guy running it made it seem like prison, and getting through like figuring out some maze."

"Kenny, you know I'm a straight shooter, so I'm going to be blunt. It's fucked up."

"How, though? Because of the responsibility?"

Henry laughs. Not a fun one, but a you-dumb-fuck one. "The inmates basically run the prison. You ever read *Lord of the Flies*?"

"No, but I've heard of it." His question matches the tone of his laugh, and I don't want to go down that road, because that point isn't really my concern. Addicts or inmates, we're pretty much the same. So, I get to what I really want to know. "Is it free?"

"Kenny? Ken-ny!" Henry's voice rises. "Please tell me that you're not considering this place as a goddamn option!"

"Chill, Henry. I'm just asking questions."

"About the wrong things! You should be thinking about what you'll do tomorrow so you won't want to use. Hell, you should be thinking about how you'll get through tonight. I know how meetings are when you're fresh out. You have a half chub for H again, and soon enough it'll be a full-fledged hard on. You cut that out right now!"

"Henry, I am." I start reciting the Serenity Prayer, thinking it might calm him down. Wrong move.

"On a scale of one to ten, how bad do you want to use right now?"

I have been forcing myself to think about anything other than that bag, but this question brings it back into focus. I know where it is and how it looks and feels, but that's normal; that's like regular people knowing about the food in their fridge and when they need to buy milk. But this question has triggered my compulsion. I *need* that bag. Now. In my hands. Inside me.

I'm going to have to tell Henry to stop asking that damn question.

"A seven. The meeting was good for me."

"How is that possible? It sounds like all you talked about was the program. Tell me the reason you're down to a seven."

Now that they've started, I can't hold the thoughts back. They flood me. *Would snorting it get me high? Is one bump really that bad? Do I know anyone with a needle?* I close my eyes and still my mind the best I can. Then I answer

Henry. "The people were good to me. They were interested in how a kid my age has been using so long."

"So you were in the limelight. That bodes real well for your need-seeking and desire for attention."

"Henry, they just had questions."

"About things that are *about* you, but aren't *good* for you."

I sigh and hear him do the same. It quiets my thoughts. Enough so that I can think to get the answers I need before it's too late.

"I was just curious, that's all. Sorry, but if I relapse, that's where I'm going. You and I both know there's a chance of that. You can't be upset with me for wanting to know what's up. I've been out of the loop for a bit."

"You have been, and I'm sorry for getting so upset. You are so incredibly vulnerable right now. The stats show how dangerous, and we both know how you love to look for those silver linings, make things seem to shine when they don't."

I remember a phone number. A kid I used to run with. *Maybe he has a needle? If he's still alive.*

"So, all I can say about the program," Henry goes on, "is don't even consider it. You asked if it's free. No, it's not free. Nothing's free. You're paying with your time. Detox is the easy part, but if you then get saddled with a group that doesn't want to go back to the real world, you're stuck. Because that's the problem with this concept, not everyone wants to change, and how the hell is someone who struggles with the same shit supposed to alter that?"

"But isn't that the point? Don't they want to kind of remove us from society?"

"Yeah, and you know what that's called, right? Genocide."

That word comes to life and sits on the floor in front of me. *Sobriety* appears out of nowhere and sits next to it. Then *Suicide* and *Overdose* slide out of my closet and join the rest. Henry talks about working steps and staying busy and thinking about a job or school, but it's just background noise. I say "Uh huh," here and there, because now the words are blinking, waiting for me to choose.

My uncle's journal sits on the end of my bed, open to those five rules. I am failing at them all. Already. Day two on the outside. I know I don't want to go back to rehab, because there really isn't one to go back to now. But staying sober is going to be as hard as everyone has always said it would be. Every fiber, working every day toward the same goal is a terribly exhausting existence. I don't want to die, but do I really want to live this life?

Death, especially by suicide, is so terrible to everyone who's ever loved you. Life, though, this clean thing that's supposed to be the goal, what's fun about it? I've screwed myself already. All that's left are meetings, and maybe community college if I can hack it. My brain's useless from all the drugs, so what awaits? A dead-end job and the crushing guilt of knowing I'm responsible for it? Fuck that.

I hang up with Henry and do not think twice before texting the number of the that kid I remembered: *It's Kenny. I'm out. New phone. Needle?*

It takes a moment for the reply to come: *Thought you were getting clean.*

I'm trying to get dirty again. I watch my text send and don't even marvel at how quickly this happened. I just want to get high.

;) Got any to spare?

No, just scratch. That's why I need to make it count.

K. I know you'll have more, later. Where you want to meet?

Same as usual. Give me an hour.

See you then.

I shouldn't be surprised at how easily old habits return. As if on autopilot, I head out to the living room and say goodnight to my parents.

"Sleep tight, bud," Dad says. "Good job today."

"Are you sure you're just tired?" Mom's eyes pry even more than the question, and part of me wants to admit what I'm about to do, but my addict is stronger and tells that part of me to go fuck itself.

"I'm good, just tired." I walk over, kiss her on the top of her head and choke down wave after wave of emotion as I head back to my room.

I lie in bed, in the dark, pretending to be asleep. I don't bother to wrestle with my conflicting thoughts because I don't have the energy. I just let them pass through until one final resolution emerges: *I am already heading down, and it's just easier to fall than it is to climb.*

I slide out my window, walk a few streets over, and my connection is waiting like I knew he would. We clasp hands and he passes me the syringe. We talk, but I can't focus on what he's saying, because as soon as that needle curled into my palm, it was like the torch had been passed, and I need to run.

I stay for another round of "No shit?" type responses, then head back home and creep into my room, quietly and stealthily, as always.

And here I am now, with a spoon, syringe, and a bag, my phone charger wrapped around my arm. It's as if the past three months never happened. It's as if I didn't mean a single word I said to the therapists and to the other patients, which somehow, I know can't be true, and yet, is, because look at me now. But I really believed it then, just like I did the first time and the second time, and during all the meetings in between. I thought I could live clean. But my addict is stronger than whoever I am, and he doesn't want me to be clean, and so that's all there is to it.

This is why I'm debating how much of this bag to use. I don't want to shoot the entire thing. My addict does. He says I can handle it. I know I've been clean too long for that to be true.

I also know which of those words, blinking at me, won out. I've never overdosed, which is shocking. I have used Narcan on runners who did OD, so it's not like I don't know what it looks like. But those were accidents, as pretty much all of them are. People who think they can handle more than they should, or just have no clue about the potency, especially with the synthetics. Then there are those who listen to their addicts because there's no other choice. Like me right now. But since I'm aware of this, it won't be an accident. If I shoot this entire bag... I guess there's only one way to find out.

The veins in my left arm are popping so hard, it looks like I work out. There are scars from my favorite injection spot, so I hone in on them, like a bullseye. This will be so easy.

I drop the white powder into the spoon, about a third of the bag, and shoot some water in from the syringe. It mixes well, so I drop in some more and add water. Half the bag is mixed and my hand wavers. This next move determines everything. I try not to think of my parents and my family and especially my uncle, but it's impossible. Even Marcus and Henry crowd my head. I have all of these supports in my life. I've yet to turn into some junkie no one will talk to, or help, or love. But I know I'm on my way. This has just been a detour.

I dump the rest of the bag in, and inject the rest of the water. I mix for a few seconds and then draw the hit. The muscle memory is on point. I tap the syringe, clear the bubbles as gently as I can so as to not lose any of the heroin.

The only light in my room comes from the lamp on my nightstand. I stare at it for a moment and envision Mom coming in and finding me. Should that be under this light? The overhead might make it too harsh, so I leave the lamp on.

I take a deep breath and insert the needle. It stings for a second, but I draw back, see blood and know I'm good to go. There is no hesitation. I inject, slowly, precisely, the whole bag up my arm. I manage to pull the syringe out just as the euphoria kicks.

My brain is split in two and my body pulses with joy. There is no pain, no fear, just this moment of ecstasy. I lie back and start to nod and it's like I've returned to a sandy beach with the Caribbean sun beating down on my naked body. I tingle and drool and my heart quickens, then thunders in my chest, a clap of sudden shock, like I've touched a live wire. My breath catches, but I'm still breathing.

My heart squeezes like it's trying to strangle itself and I pull at my chest. My breath catches again, this time for longer. My face tingles and grows hot. I'm suffocating.

My throat is closed and straining to open. All of my muscles are taut. I'm on my bed, losing my life, while inside my head all I can feel is the warmth of light.

5

If this is death, then all the books and movies come close, but not exact. Because here I am, out of my body, looking at the scene of my crime. My body is breathless, mouth gasping, achieving nothing. My face is bright red from the exertion, and all of my muscles are taut. Then my body gives up, and the me that is looking on flickers. On the bed, my arm collapses, and the spoon strikes the lampshade, toppling it to the floor. The bulb breaks and we are thrust into darkness.

Footsteps charge down the hall, but the door is opened gently. "Kenny?" Mom says. "You all right?"

The hallway light allows me to see my body. This is what I'd hoped to avoid, but apparently, I can't even overdose correctly.

The door opens wider. "Kenny!" Dad's voice makes the me watching cower, and then the overhead light is switched on and they both scream.

My skin is blue and seems to be darkening.

Mom goes to my side and screams my name and slaps my face. Dad runs from the room but returns in seconds with an armful of Narcan. How many times have they prepared for this?

"Call 911!" Dad barks to Mom as he slips the wrapper off the Narcan spray.

Mom's entire body shakes as she pulls the phone from her pocket and puts the call on speaker.

Dad doesn't wait for instructions from the operator; he jams the tip of the nasal spray into my nose and hits the plunger.

The me who is watching feels a pull, like I'm being lifted out of a chair, but I fall back into it.

The 911 operator asks if I've started breathing. Mom says, "No," and Dad is unwrapping the second Narcan, just as the operator tells him to give me another one, if they have it.

Before he administers the second spray, I notice how much stiffer my body has become. I'm a light-blue mannequin.

Dad administers, and I feel the tug again, stronger this time, enough to pull me to my feet.

"Don't worry, paramedics are on their way," the operator says, but my parents are quiet, watching, waiting for me to come back to life.

Nothing happens. Not to my body. The me that is watching sits back down and I feel a warmth spread through me. A noise, but maybe only the sensation of a noise calls to me, and I turn and have the desire to go toward it, but the direction isn't to the left or right or back, it's elsewhere, and I can't make myself move.

"Do another!" Mom screams. The operator asks what's going on, but in response, Mom drops the phone and grabs my body in an embrace. I feel that, too. Her warm tears on my neck, the strength of her arms. Then the third spray hits and the noise from elsewhere stops. Everything stops. There is no sound, only sensation, and the me who is watching is propelled through wherever I was and back to myself.

Whether it's the Narcan or the collective wish from my parents that I live again, I suck in air like I've returned from the depth of the ocean.

The paramedics arrive and Dad lets them in and it's flat-out commotion. I'm moved from my bed onto a gurney. An IV is put into my arm and a mask goes on my face, and my parents are unable to look me in the eye.

I'm wheeled outside, into the night, and flashing lights bounce off the homes of my neighbors, some of whom are out and watching. My parents are silent, holding each other, not speaking to me. They don't ask questions of the paramedics, either, which strikes me as odd, but then, like the resurfacing, I'm back to the realization of what this means. I've failed to die, and now must live according to the government's standards, and neither my parents nor I have a say.

The paramedics load me into the back of the van and shut the doors.

The ambulance rumbles over streets and all is quiet. No one speaks to me or to each other, so I take a stab at one more chance. "Are we going to St. Jude's?" I ask, because that's the hospital we always go to.

The paramedic shakes his head and then speaks directly into my ear. "You belong to the government now. Your care will occur at Ward 15."

I nod and lie back. There's nothing else to do but wait for whatever the program truly is.

In the dark of night and the scattered street lights, Ward 15 looks like an old school. We enter through the back, like a delivery to the kitchen. But once inside, medical staff greet me in their scrubs and the paramedics talk to them about me. But no one from the staff asks me my name or my date of birth. They don't speak to me at all.

They transition me from the paramedics' gurney to one of their own and then move me from the bay, down the hall, and into a wide-open room. There are curtains, carving out spaces here and there, but along the walls are medical hookups for what seems to be an endless supply of beds. If this was a school, then I'm in a cafeteria, stripped bare of tables and refurbished to accommodate hundreds.

I'm moved into one of the curtained sections and then a nurse finally takes vitals and notes my chart. In the typical drill, the next step is sedation and fluids. I'll sleep for a few days and wake up sore and groggy, like I've gotten over the flu, and then detox would be over.

But I look at the saline bag on the IV stand. That's all there is. Unless I missed it, they injected nothing to put me out. In fact, I'm starting to wake up. The nurse slides my chart into the foot of my bed, strips off his gloves, and goes to step through the curtain, clearly done.

I force myself to speak. "Wait! What's going on?"

The nurse turns back, looking bothered by the question. "This ain't your first rodeo, you know what's going on."

The fact that I've just come back from the dead and am now in some warehouse of a facility has actually changed the game for me, but I can tell arguing is futile by the way the nurse purses his lips, so I say, "Detox?"

"Yup. In a few hours, you're going to feel pretty damn terrible, so I'd rest up if you can."

I wait for more, but he says nothing. Then I hear the familiar sounds of other patients around me. Their groaning, their requests for a nurse, for water. I sniff and smell vomit and shit. This is not normal.

"What about?" I point at the IV, trying to get the words out.

"Sedation?" the nurse fills in the blank for me.

I nod.

"No. That's not how we do things here at Ward 15. Welcome to the new protocol of addiction recovery."

His face is neutral—pursed lips gone—and yet the waking part of me feels as if there's pleasure in what he's helping me understand. He cups my knee.

"I know you're probably used to a lot different treatment, but that treatment clearly hasn't worked or you wouldn't be here. Don't look so surprised."

"Okay. So what's next?"

"Oh, that's easy. You're going to suffer, and we're not going to fix that. But we'll keep you alive so that you'll remember." He pats my knee and walks out, leaving the curtain open wide enough for me to see a section of the room, but I'm too paralyzed with fear to call him back to close it. Either fear, or the realization that it wouldn't matter how much I pleaded, I'm expected to endure it all.

***

I think I've figured it out. On the outskirts of town, where it starts to bleed into the city, there's this old school. When I was little and had friends, not just user buddies, we'd drive past it on our way to the museum or to the enormous bookstore, and we'd try to convince each other that the school was haunted. The windows were boarded up and the concrete stairs leading to the main entrance of the brick building were crumbling. The grounds looked as if nature was trying to reclaim the space. What used to be a parking lot, was cracked pavement and weeds. We'd tell stories of who died in there and how. Old nuns, and later, teens who'd snuck in and were scared to death. The place was filled with ghosts.

I never realized how prescient we were.

This is that old school. It has to be. The ceiling I've been staring at all night, which is now being bathed in sunlight, has cracks that have been patched over, and water stains that are seeping through the new paint. What I saw last night was the refurbished exterior to a place I conjured as a place of specters.

They cried and screamed all around me last night. I shook then, but out of fear, unlike the gentle tremors that have now begun. I look for a call button, but there isn't one. I have a heart monitor on and know I could tear that off and it should alert. But what if it doesn't? Worse, what if it does and they don't come or don't care?

If I just had an Oxy, or even just a bump of H. Shit, I'd settle for a Vicodin.

My feet bounce to their own rhythm, as if they're trying to run away. A thought I haven't considered. If I can get out of this bed, then maybe I can find out.

I swing my legs over the side but am immediately doubled over by a cramp. The scream unfurls without my permission. I hear its echo, or another patient responding in kind.

The curtain swooshes open and a nurse walks in. Not the one from last night. This one's eyes are underscored with dark pools, almost as if she's an addict and not staff.

"You okay?" she asks and moves my legs back onto the bed.

"No. I'm shaking and I just got this cramp. Could you please give me something? I didn't sleep at all last night."

She laughs. "You probably won't sleep again for a while." The nurse checks my IV bag, marks something on my chart. "So, I'm just supposed to lie here? Can't I take a walk? What if I need to go to the bathroom?" My words feel like I'm spitting venom, they come out so strong and forceful.

The nurse turns an icy glare over me. "Yes, you are going to *just* lie here. If you can walk on your own, go for it. No one here is going to help you, not until you've detoxed. So, most likely, you get out of that bed, you'll fall and end up on the floor. It's colder down there, too. The shakes haven't kicked in yet. You're going to want the blanket, and the bedpan."

"That's it? Just torture the shit out of me? Out of all of us? Is this supposed to be like scared straight for addicts or some shit? Cuz I'm not scared."

She moves to the bed and pats my face. "You will be."

Then she's gone, and as if on cue, tremors take hold of my body.

***

I have no idea when it is. Not time, not day. All I know is that my knees and my hips and my back feel like they're trying to climb out of my body. Sleep refuses to come to me. I nod and snap awake and the nightmare continues to unfold. I roll from one side to the next, hoping it will help. Nothing helps. Heroin would help. A nice big hit would be perfect. Or having died from the last shot I took would have been perfect. But no, I was saved...for this.

Nurses come and go and have tried to make me sip juice and soup. Whatever I can get down comes right back up. They hung another bag next to the saline and I was momentarily overjoyed that they finally relented to sedating me.

"It's dextrose, honey. You don't get to die on account of not having enough energy. This should keep you going."

If I could get my hands to stop shaking, or really, my body to cooperate in any coordinated way, I'd strangle myself with the IV tubes. But I lack the strength, in spite of the sugar water. I have always lacked the strength, and I guess this is their way of reminding me.

***

Fluids are passing out of everywhere. I'm pissing out my ass and throwing up at the same time. No one seems to care. It splatters to the ground and a nurse pops his or her head in, but that's it. They're waiting for something, but I don't know what.

"Could someone please help me?" I try to scream, but I'm too weak to scream. It comes out as a muted plea to my pillow. "Help," I say, "please help." But no one hears or comes and my stomach knots up and I'm puking and shitting all over again.

My eyes burn and my throat is on fire, but there's no water to drink and no one to tend to me. I shake and shake and the thin blanket they gave me does nothing. "Heroin," I say. "Fucking heroin." My brain scrambles to figure out what comes next, but instead a void of thought occurs. I don't know if I'm begging for the drug or cursing it.

"That's right, man, fucking heroin," someone says nearby. Another patient, or am I hallucinating?

"She made you her bitch, too, huh?" the voice asks.

For a second, I consider not answering, but then realize there is no point. Hallucination or not, he's right. "Yeah, she did. You?"

My voice is weak but must carry, because he answers. "You know it. Man, I'm just starting to shake. This is gonna suck."

I laugh. I don't know where it comes from because there's not a damn thing funny about this, but my neighbor laughs as well. "Just wait until you start shitting yourself," I say. "Liquid gold."

My neighbor laughs at this. "*Liquid gold*. Man, I hear you. They ain't knocking us out, are they?"

"No," I say. Then, "Hey, do you know what day it is?"

"I think it's like Wednesday. No, no, I OD'd on Wednesday. It's gotta be like Thursday or something. How long you been here?"

It takes a minute to figure it out. "Late Saturday night, Sunday morning, somewhere round there."

"And you've been in that bed the whole time?"

I look around me, at the utter filth that I have become. But I'm not shaking anymore. "Haven't gotten up once."

"So you really are just a puddle of shit over there?"

"Yeah, but I think I kicked it."

"For real? Without being knocked out?"

"Yeah. I mean, I passed out, I think, but they kept me up."

"Oh, you up now." There's a pause. "All right, well, I better find a comfy position to die in. I'm Mike, by the way. You know, if I make it out of here and to whatever's next."

"You will. I'm Kenny, man. Good luck."

"Thanks, Kenny. I have a feeling I'm going to need it." Mike's words jar together at the end. His jaw must be shaking now. Damn is he in for a ride.

The privacy curtain opens and the nurse I first saw looks at me over his facemask. "Well, look who survived."

I don't bother to try and sit up. "If you call this survival," I say.

"Oh, and you're witty. You know I could let you lie there another day if you want."

I go to speak but the nurse cracks up. "You see, I can be witty, too." He moves to the bed and looks down at me. "Anyway, I can't have you stink up the space your new friend Mike is about to occupy." He says this loud enough for Mike to hear.

"Th-th-ank you, S-sir," Mike manages.

"Oh, he's a big boy, too. It's going to get epic up in here." The nurse rolls me to one side with his gloved hands, untucks the bed and then rolls me to my other side and does the same over there, and then in a quick pop, the bed sheet has been removed and I'm lying on the cold vinyl mattress. He places a clean blanket over me because I've started to shake.

"Don't worry, you just cold. That's normal. The poison's out of your system. I just need to get some vitals and then we'll get you cleaned up and some food in your belly. That sound good?"

My stomach growls at the word food, but I ignore it. "And then what?"

"Well, that answer depends on a lot of things. But the easiest answer is: you start praying."

"What?"

"Not like as in we gonna send you to church," the nurse says while rolling a thermometer over my forehead and temple. "As in, you need to start asking God to give you a good ten to work with, because if He don't, you ain't ever leaving here."

6

I'm riding in a wheelchair, because when my nurse swung my legs over the bed and asked me to stand, I almost fell. My legs are far too weak. While we travel, I get a glimpse of the detox room. If the closed curtains equal patients, then there are at least thirty more losing fluids and their minds. No wonder they just leave the clean up until the end. It's all they'd be doing otherwise.

"Is this the old school?" I ask my nurse. "The one at the edge of the city?"

He nods. "Yup. I had an uncle who went through here before they re-zoned and it got boarded up. PS 15."

So, it is no surprise then, when the kitchen bleeds into a hallway that wraps to the back gym. My nurse brings me to the locker room and then into the showers. I hate P.E. almost as much as I hate rehab.

"I'll help you as much as you need, but it's best if you try and stand. Use the railings and you'll be all right," my nurse says, and then unties the gown I've been lying in, which is basically crusted to me. He helps me stand and the gown doesn't fall off.

"Well, this is gross," I say.

"Wait till it warms up under the water." My nurse turns on the closest shower, one of about twenty in a wide-open space. A metal safety railing runs halfway up the wall, under the nozzles, throughout the room. I imagine this is what a geriatric shower might look like, but I'm pretty sure those retirement homes have private stalls.

He helps me stand and I wait awhile until the dizziness passes and then I shuffle toward the water. There's a slight lip at the edge, and stepping over it makes my leg muscles feel like they're cracking into shards of glass. I take a deep breath, grab the railing, and shuffle beneath the water.

"I got you if you feel like you're going to fall or slip, but I ain't no mind reader so give a holler, you know."

I nod, but am at a loss for words because of how extraordinary the water feels. It's the perfect temperature. At first it gives me goose bumps, but they fade and a warmth passes through me. It's similar to that heroin rush, but not nearly as potent. Not even close. And now that I've thought about my girl, she's all I can think about. I know at some point I'm going to go from here to a therapist or something and then onto the ward. I have no clue how many kids are here, or how many guards or how it is all structured—beyond whatever the group of ten looks like—but I'm pretty positive that someone will be able to get contraband. Even if it's just a Klonopin, it'll help take the edge off. But I know what I really want, and that she'll have to wait.

The gown is now soaked and hangs heavily from my shoulders. In spite of it being untied, it still doesn't fall. "Little help with this," I say, and my nurse comes over.

"Move a bit so the water's hitting the top. I'll peel."

I do and feel the gown saturate around my chest, and then the sucking sensation as my nurse takes the gown off, like dead skin after a sunburn. He pulls it away and lets it fall to the ground behind me. It sounds like a body dropping, a noise I've heard too many times.

"You all right, Kenny. You look like something's up?"

I grip the railing even tighter. "Is it just guys here? Or is this co-ed?"

My nurse's laugh echoes throughout the stall. "Oh, I see, player. You already thinking 'bout girls. I feel you." He taps my hand with a bottle. "Take some of this first and clean that body. You look like a dirty-ass piece of toilet paper."

He squeezes the body soap into my hand. It smells like mint. "You're just saying that because I'm white." I smile. It's the second joke I've made since I've been here and it feels good to joke again.

"While this may be true," my nurse says, "I'd say the same to a brother."

I suds and say, "I don't know if that makes it better, but whatever. Girls, yes or no?"

He laughs. "Trading one addiction for another."

"It's not like that." Even I feel how hollow my words are.

"Well, I guess that's good, then, 'cuz it's just bros up in here. The girls' ward is elsewhere. Part of the protocol."

"All right. Probably better that way." I wasn't hoping for any action or anything, just a lay of the land. It's starting to crystalize.

My nurse opens up a tiny bottle of shampoo. "Bend over." I do and he squirts it on. "You might see some of your friends, here, though."

I scrub my head, digging into my scalp. It hasn't felt this good to get so clean in a long time. "I wouldn't say I have friends. But, you're right, a lot of the people I ran with are stupid enough to end up here."

"I wouldn't say they were stupid for getting clean."

"No, it's more like they're stupid for waiting this long. Because now—"

"Now what?"

"Now it's the real deal, right? I mean, before, at my other centers, they had us detox while sedated, and after, they treated us all nice and brought us snacks and we talked about our feelings all the time." I rinse the suds off my head.

"And it didn't work." My nurse says this as a matter of fact.

"No. But does this method?"

He grabs a towel from a rack in the corner and then shuts off my water. Before he hands me the towel he says, "Do you want to get clean?"

I'm dripping wet, free of the grime of the past few days, and the irony is not lost on me, but I answer honestly. "I don't know."

My nurse hands me the towel. "Then, to your question, I offer you the same answer you just gave me."

I wrap the towel over my head and wish I could hide in its folds and not face myself for the rest of my life.

I get dry and my body feels infinitely better. Then my nurse hands me tighty whiteies, knee-high, white socks, a light blue T-shirt, a bright blue set of sweat pants and sweat shirt, and a pair of black, slide sandals. I feel like I've stepped back into second grade.

"Every group gets a color. It's how we keep track of things. You'll learn to love looking like a blueberry."

I shake my head. "This is part of the system, isn't it? You're demoralizing us."

"If you want to walk around naked, go ahead." He pauses. "But I think that's gonna be a bit more demoralizing."

I look my nurse in the eye. "Did you just make a shrinkage joke?"

"Nope. You implied that."

I grab the clothing from his hands. "Oh, no, you know you did." With his help, I dress, and indeed feel like a blueberry.

He directs me back into the wheelchair and then says, "You get to clean that outfit once a week, so do your best not to get anything on it. If you get nasty on a Tuesday and laundry isn't until Friday, you gonna have to deal with that."

I say nothing as he wheels me out of the locker room and back into the hall. He's proven my premise correct. This is going to be more like prison than it is rehab.

We end up outside a set of doors, behind which comes a strong aroma of food. "If the cafeteria is your detox room, then what's this?"

"They had a big-ass conference room next to the cooking classes room or something, so they converted it." He swipes a card at the pad next to the door and it beeps. He did this before we went into the locker room, but I was too lost to ask, then. I do now.

"Every door locked?"

"Every one. Including your bedroom."

The door pops open and he wheels me into a scaled down cafeteria and heads turn. Other patients, dressed in blue, and black, and yellow, are here. Some have a nurse, some don't. I look around and the cafeteria ladies smile at me. "Where are the guards?" I ask.

"There aren't any."

I remember the conversation from the meeting I attended, about the prisoners running the place. "Like, at all?"

"No, but where they are, you don't want to be." He claps his hands. "For now, let's get you some food. You'll learn all about the program soon enough."

I eat my first meal in days, and combined with the sweat suit, makes me feel like a geriatric patient. Applesauce and pudding, with some crackers and string cheese. The only beverage option is water, so I drink that. All of it is bland, government supplied, and off label, but my stomach loves every second of it.

While I eat, my nurse hangs with the other nurses. I look around the room at the patients. Some look as frail as I know I am, while others look like they've never been strung out a day in their lives. It also looks like the white kids are a minority, which is new for me, because at other facilities that wasn't the case. Most times, everybody was white, except for some of the staff.

When you do drugs, you meet all sorts of people, so I have no beef with anyone white, brown, or black, so long as they don't mess with me. Outside, on the streets, people fuck with you all the time, especially dealers. Rehab usually has only one or two assholes, though, and as I look around, I don't know if there's one in this crowd or not, so I'm trying to remember faces as best I can.

"Hey! Hey, yo! What you looking at?"

The food in my stomach feels like a bowling pin. The questions are coming at me from a black kid in blue, two tables over.

I swallow my fear. "Right now, you."

I wait for the pop of anger, for him to get up and charge me, but he tilts his head back and laughs. The kids next to him, one black, one brown, laugh along and nudge him with their elbows. The first kid mutters, "You," and laughs again. Then he looks at me. "Stop looking and come over. You one of us." He pops his sweatshirt for emphasis.

If the rumors of the treatment are right, then I'm looking at one third of my crew. I stand, but immediately feel dizzy and sit back down. My head swims and I have to close my eyes. I hear movement and expect my nurse to be checking my pulse.

"Have a sip, yo. This water tastes like ass, but it'll help."

I open my eyes and the blue crew has come to my table. The first kid I was talking to holds the straw to me. I sip from it, feeling a mix of embarrassment and relief. When I lean back, they all look on.

"You just get clean?" the other black kid asks.

"Yeah, literally just came from the shower, so I'm weak as hell. Thanks for helping me out."

They all nod in unison, more as if they're a set of triplets than three guys who are on the ward together.

"You guys used to run together?" I ask.

They all shake their heads, and the first black kid says, "No, man. We ain't known each other till we ended up here."

"How long ago was that?"

The first kid points to himself, "I've been here the longest, 'bout three months. I'm Rashad by the way." He points at the other black kid. "Devon, you been here almost two months?"

"Yeah," Devon says, "livin' the dream."

Rashad points at the brown kid. "And don't mind Ramirez too much. Dude says like eight words a day. But you been here just over a month, right?"

Ramirez smiles shyly and nods.

"So that's us," Rashad says. "There's five more for you to meet, but don't sweat it, we basically all the same. So who's you?"

"Right, awesome to meet you all. I'm Kenny."

They laugh together and I don't understand until Rashad says, "Two of our crew got released two weeks ago and we was betting who we'd get. I think Big James had *Basic White Kid named Ken* or something like that. Man, he's spot on. Look at you."

I liked these guys for a minute, now I'm not so sure.

"Oh, man," Devon says, "check his face. He don't find that funny."

"My bad, Kenny. I'm forgetting what it's like to be new here. You don't know what's what. We just playing, no worries. Big James is like the best brother you'll ever know. We all good, just need shit to pass the time is all."

"Okay," I say, but have no clue if I mean it. "Could you do me a favor? Could you explain how things work? Like real simple, because my brain is still moving slow."

"No doubt," Rashad says. "So here it go. When I came in, I joined a blue group of nine dudes, so we make up ten, total. Just like you doing now, 'cept we got two released, so we waiting on one more after you. Right now, everybody in the group is praying that the boys that got released stay clean, 'cuz if they stay sober for one month, everybody that was in the group gets five points per person. There are other ways to get points, like doing good shit and whatnot, but once you get one hundred points, you get released. Unless, they don't stay clean. That shit's everything."

I tease this around for a minute. "So what happens if they don't stay clean?"

The three look at each other and their faces turn into disgusted scowls. Devon says, "Then those points are subtracted."

"How would they know? I mean, if he moved away or something."

Devon leans across the table and spreads the skin at the side of his neck. A tiny square bumps out from between his fingers. "You see that shit? It's like they use for dogs. Scan it and they know who we are. Except this one also have GPS. They got your ass." He lets go of his neck. "You got one already and don't even know it."

I feel my neck, expecting nothing, that Devon is playing me, that he's got some weird mole or something, some birthmark, and he's been using this story for years. But no, I feel the same square in my own neck. My heart starts pounding and my head is light again.

"Drink," Ramirez says, his voice a whisper, but something about the intensity makes it louder. I'm not sure how he knew, but he's right, I need a drink. I sip and the cold water feels good. But my brain still surges with questions.

Rashad holds up a hand. "Slow it down, Kenny. There's a lot to learn and even more time to learn it. You're going to be here a while, so just chill. We got you."

I nod. "Thanks. I'm just—my mind's just—"

"Totally fucked," Devon says. "You wouldn't be here if it weren't."

"But you all seem so good, so clean. Aren't you craving?"

"Every goddamn day," Rashad says. "But this shit—" he circles his finger "—it gets you correct quick. 'Cuz now that you know you got a chip in your neck and who knows what else in you they ain't told you about, plus the fact that dudes' lives are riding on your ass, it changes you." He pauses, looks at Devon and Ramirez. "Least I hope it does."

7

I have a million questions to still ask, but my nurse comes over and says, "Glad you met your crew, but it's time to get going."

It's weird, I didn't hear a bell or an announcement. All the other places I've been in ran on a schedule—some tighter than others—and always someone or something announced what was next. But Rashad and the rest of my blue crew grab their trays at my nurse's words and bring them to the bins for the lunch ladies. The same is true for the other patients. They dump food and then line up at the door. I'm wheeled into line after I've taken care of my tray and my crew fits in behind me.

I turn back to my nurse. "Do I go onto the ward now?"

"Yup. You'll get your room assignment and meet the head of the ward. Then you'll have a meeting. Don't worry, you'll get a schedule and a better understanding. Just sit back and enjoy the ride." He cracks a smile, but I don't join in. We're moving now, and in spite of how comfortable I feel, I know not to trust my emotions to stay in one place for long. Except craving. I'll always be craving.

The line moves out the door and takes a left, winding down a long hallway in the opposite direction I came. The building has such a school vibe, in spite of the retrograde, it's unnerving. That same floor tile, that's like scattered rocks, is everywhere, and up and down the hall are the remnant outlines of message corkboards. The classroom doors are gone, though, and as we come to the end of this section of hall, the group in yellow splits off. At the end of the hall is another double door with an access pad. Someone on the inside lets the boys in, and they walk through the door before a buzzing noise is audible and then the lock bolts into place. There is no sound from their ward, and I can only imagine the extent of soundproofing that's gone in.

I watch the group in black do the same, silently, wordlessly, almost as if they're drugged. And when we come to yet another capped off hallway, it's our turn. My nurse waves at someone who isn't wearing scrubs, so I'm guessing he isn't a nurse. That guy opens the door and I enter with the rest. They split off, however, but not without telling me they'll see me in a bit.

43

The door locks behind me, and now it's the non-nurse guy, and me. Sunlight pools in from the one side of the hall, and it's the first indication of the weather outside. Seeing it turns something in me and I feel the prickling sensation of tears.

"Welcome, Kenny, I'm counselor Tom Hobson. I run the ward." He is all smiles and extends his hand to me. I take it and shake with what little strength I have. "That's a good grip. Seems like breakfast served you well." He laughs and the nurse laughs and I look past him to the ward. The other five guys in blue, who I've yet to meet, are looking on, checking me out. When did they have breakfast?

Counselor Tom gets in my way, so I can only see him. "I'm sure you have a thousand and one questions, and I guarantee you that we'll answer them all. Okay?"

I nod.

"Good. For now, let's see if you can walk. Feel free to use the wall for support."

I expect them to let me stand on my own, but the two men hoist me up by my armpits and lean me against the wall. I get a head rush. Then my nurse is clicking the brakes off and says, "Peace, Kenny." He unlocks the door and is gone before I can say, "But I can't walk."

"That's beside the point," Counselor Tom says. "You don't have far to go. Anyway, you won't be able to walk if we keep you in that chair. Time to stretch."

I hope they have medical staff on the ward or some that are a phone call away, because I'm not feeling like I can do anything but fall down and sleep on the floor. Tom, though, gets my arm around his shoulders and starts walking. I keep up by using one hand on the wall.

Fortunately, he goes slow. I struggle to move my feet, and my hips and back scream with every movement. But I hear voices from the ward.

"Yo, check 'em."

"You got it, son."

"One foot in front of the other."

"Just don't fall, Tom likes white meat."

Tom stops at this last comment and looks around. He clearly has no idea who said it, because he mumbles to himself and then resumes helping me hobble down the hall.

The guys stand in their doorways of what seem like tiny rooms. My best guess is that they chopped up a classroom to create them. The guys don't jeer or crack jokes at my expense. They're positive, yelling, "You got this, Kenny." I'm guessing Rashad and the others leaked my name.

We take a few dozen more steps and I'm beginning to use the wall less. Another dozen and I ask Tom if I can try a few on my own. He drops my arm and I walk the first steps I've taken in days. There's a booming round of applause and I can't help but smile.

"Nice work, Kenny, but stop here."

"Why?"

"We're at your room." Tom nods his head, indicating that I should go inside.

Instead of the bunkbed setup that I expected, there are two single beds, fitted with dark gray blankets and white sheets. A single pillow rests at the top. There's a window looking onto the courtyard, and other than two night stands and a small foot locker, there's nothing else in the room.

I look to Tom. "Which bed is mine?"

"Pick. We've had two leave, so you'll have a roommate in a day or two, I bet."

So Rashad and Devon weren't lying. I move to the bed on the right, for no other reason than its easier to walk in that direction. I sit and the bed's hard as a rock, but I don't care because I'm worn out from those baby steps.

"Good," Tom says. "Sit tight, because I have something for you. I'll be right back."

I'm sure he has all sorts of fun pamphlets for me to read, and possibly contracts to sign. My other facilities always had behavior contracts about not doing this or agreeing to doing that. I always signed them and then went right back to doing whatever the hell I wanted. But here, there's no movement. No one's walking around, popping in to say hey. There's just a blank and empty hallway before me, and the tiny room where I now live. The door is open, a pocket one that is probably automated to lock and unlock. Just like prison. At least I have a window.

Voices bounce up and down the hall, but nothing sounds important. Just guys talking. If I could stand, I could join in, but for right now, I'll just sit and absorb. Because this, in spite of being a mix of torture and incarceration, already feels different. I don't know if this is good or bad, but I'm certain I'll know by the end of the day. I go to lean back on the bed—whatever Tom's grabbing is taking forever—but when I do, there's a camera eyeballing me. It's one of those ceiling-mount, 360-degree, spheres, encased in a protective glass. I hear it whir. Camera's in the room? That's new, and creepy as hell. How often are the on? Day? Night? Constantly? Are they recording?

Tom comes back. "Sorry for the delay, I had to answer a quick email." He sees me looking up. "Oh, you've found our eyes in the sky, huh?"

"So it is a camera?"

"Yup." Tom raps it with a knuckle. "It's equipped with night-vision and is always running." He looks at me. "You can understand our need to keep you safe."

Yes and no. Last time I was behind a closed door I almost died, sure, but how am I going to do that in here?

Before I can say anything, Tom has something he's holding out to me. "Here, this might make you feel a little better."

I take it and turn over the notebook in my hands. It's my uncle's journal. "How did you—" I don't finish my question.

"We allow one personal item and your parents chose this." He sits on the other bed. "I can understand. Having an uncle succeed is a great motivator, and his words of how he achieved such can provide fantastic guidance."

As he speaks, I begin to flip through. I stop, though, when I notice something that wasn't there before. Black marker covers whole sections of pages, and lines here and there. There's a term for what they've done, and I fish around in my mind for it.

"Clearly, we need to read anything that comes through our doors, and your uncle's ideas, well, some of them don't fit our protocol, so we had to make sure they did."

"So you redacted them?" There, I found the word. "This is his original. You've ruined it."

Tom seems to count before speaking. "We've only done our job. I'm sorry that your parents didn't think to send you a copy." His tone is calm, but he's clearly trying to contain the anger in his voice. He's one of those guys, whose buttons are so obvious, it's nearly impossible not to push them.

"What if I were to tell you that he's a writer and he's going to get this published?" I hold up Uncle Theo's journal, but it doesn't feel like it adds strength to the argument.

Tom lets out a little chuckle. "If that's the case, then maybe he's already turned it into a manuscript and that's why he could send the original."

He's got me there. I place the journal on the bed and look out the window. I could be at home right now, reading the original, watching TV, wasting time online, anything but this. So why did I choose this? That's right, I didn't. My addict did. And yet I'm the one paying. I'm already sick of myself.

"Listen, Kenny. This place will work. Our ideas aren't off-the-wall, we're just very restrictive. It's the one thing we believe does the trick."

"Until we're out of here, then you have no sway."

Tom doesn't answer right away, but when he does, there's that hint of anger, or malice, beneath. "Well, let's see about that. Group's in five minutes. We'll come get you then." He stands up and leaves and the door stays open. Even though he hasn't told me, I know not to go through it. I look up at the camera and then around the room and then back out to the courtyard. I'm clean. That should be enough. For some rehabs it is. But they never worked. And outpatient therapy was a joke. I'll give this a try, see if the counseling here is any good. Maybe they'll have some fantastic support. If not, I'll...

I can't finish the idea. There really isn't an *if not* option anymore.

Rashad and the rest of the blue crew show up five minutes later outside my door. "Time to go, Kenny," Rashad says, and I stand. I find it strange that he doesn't come in, and I also find it strange that they just believe that I'll be able to walk when only a short time ago, I was in a wheelchair.

I get up and manage to shuffle out to the hall. Devon and Ramirez both give me a quick nod. The rest eye me, but no one says anything. "Just get in line and we'll lead the way."

"Is it just us?" I ask before moving to the end.

"Yup. You'll see."

I fall in line and follow them down the hall to the locked doors, which buzz and click and then open. Before we pass through, I notice a monitor. It has our names and then numbers after it. I scan for mine and I have zero.

But Ramirez has eighty and Devon ninety. Rashad is on top with ninety-five. This seems like a tally of the point system Rashad was talking about, but there's no time to ask about it, because we take a left and then stand outside another room. It's unmarked, and I've yet to see one guard. I've stolen, robbed people, and have even threatened to kill. I doubt I'm the only one in this group who can say that, and yet we're allowed to be together with no supervision. Then I look up. There are cameras everywhere.

The door buzzes and we file in. A goateed man in glasses says hello to each person as they walk by. When it's my turn he extends his hand. "And you must be Kenneth."

I shake his hand and say, "Kenny's fine."

"All right, Kenny. I'm John, and this is group. We have it every day at this time, so ask any questions as we move through. Okay?"

"Sure," I say, and then grab a seat next to this enormous white kid.

He looks at me with slit eyes. "I'm Big James. And you're Basic Ken, right?"

"Kenny works."

Big James squirms in his seat. "I hate these chairs, Kenny. Case you haven't noticed, I'm a big fucker. Like four bills. How is it that you and I both get the same space for our asses? Mine's like three of yours." We both look down, and sure enough, his ass is spilling every which way over the chair.

"The government," I say.

James laughs. "You don't even know how right you are, but you'll find out quick. This place is so simple, yet so scary at the same time."

I want James to keep talking, to explain, but John stands at the front and everyone shuts up. It's shocking.

"Today, as you know, we have a new member. We'll get to Kenny's story in a moment, but first, let's start with our mantra."

I'm ready to say the Serenity Prayer, which I think was the beginning to like every meeting I've ever been to, period. But they don't say that.

"Stay clean by any means," comes out of every mouth, and then John asks, "What if you see your old dealer?"

The group says, "Stay clean."

"What if the itch is so strong, you're ready to die or shoot?"

"Any means."

John pauses and seems to let the echo of the answer dissipate before speaking again. "Because if you use, who are you hurting?"

"All ten," comes the reply.

"Do you want to be that one in ten?"

"No, sir!"

"Do you remember what happens if you leave here but have to come back?"

"Yes, sir!"

This feels more militant than I expected, and of course I'm wondering what does happen if you fall off the wagon. Most places make it seem like a possibility, like all you have to do is accept the mistake and get back on the wagon. But just make damn sure you stay on. That doesn't seem to be the case, here.

John, as if reading my thoughts, powers up the projector above us. It displays his computer screen, and a grid of the city. In the bottom left corner are faces and names of people I have never met. They're kids, like us, and they have numbers associated with their identification. Those numbers are on the grid.

"Let's look at Frank," John says, and then taps the screen. We zoom in on Frank. "Here's his activity for the past twenty-four hours." A green line goes into motion, moving along the grid, to what looks like a bus stop, and then a school, and then back to the bus stop and then home.

"Perfect," John says, and everyone nods along.

"Why's it perfect?" I ask James.

"Oh, he just got released. Looks like he's being good. School and back, that's good."

Makes sense, but I ask, "He could have scored at school, or on the bus?"

James swivels as best he can to look me straight on. "Check it," he says and points at the screen, just as John is pulling up something in Frank's profile.

"And as you'll see," John says, "not a trace of any drugs in his system."

"How the hell does he know that?" I say.

Big James taps on my neck, in the exact spot where the chip has been placed. "As you can tell, that ain't just some GPS."

I stare at the screen as John runs through the next few kids. It's all the same. We watch where they go and whether or not they've used, and with each kid, there's a sigh of relief. It's messed up, because usually group is spent talking about our addiction and what we need to do to stay straight and to come to terms with the reasons why we use—if we even know. But this, this is totally different. This is tracking and performance and dependency on others. Yet, as I watch the faces around me, and the relief that washes over them as each good report comes back, it's as if I'm looking at users getting a fix. Their faces relax, as do their shoulders. They lean back and talk to each other. Laughter pops around the room. They're downright high off this.

"Do all the groups do this?" I ask James.

"Yeah. We each get time with counselors. We *track and talk*, that's the term."

"And this works? Do you still feel like using?"

James raises his hand.

"Yes, James," John says.

"Time to talk. Kenny is confused."

John smiles and it reminds me a beetle closing up on itself.

"Of course, he is." He looks at me. "In case it isn't obvious, these are patients for whom some of this group depends. I know Rashad and Devon and Ramirez gave you the basics of the program, so here's the rest."

"How did you know that?" I ask before thinking through the possibilities.

John shakes his head. "You've seen the cameras, right?"

I nod.

"They have microphones, too."

The room laughs at this, and it's weird as hell. Someone says, "I wish they could understand what I'm saying in my sleep. My dreams are whack."

"So, no twelve steps, no therapy?" I ask.

John blinks behind his glasses. "You sound disappointed."

"No, no, it's not that, just trying to understand."

"That makes sense." John looks around the room. "José, could you explain?"

A brown boy stands and waves. "Hey, Kenny. So, it's like this. The government took over therapy because the rest don't work. Sitting around and talking about things and lying to the staff about your progress is nonsense. Most of us just get kicked out after insurance stops paying anyway, and then we relapse and if we're lucky, don't die. This costs so much money and is so useless, they've devised this program, One in Ten." He pauses, looks at John, who gives him a thumbs-up.

"I know it's been mostly explained to you, and so here's how it works." He points to the screen. "We track everyone who is released for thirty days. If they stay clean, those of us connected to them—because we were counted in their ten—get points for each one. Also, if we do other things on the ward when asked, we gain points, so within three months or so, if you've been clean and behaved, and those you supported here are out in the world and sober for a month—which is the most critical time—you get to go out and join them, and by staying clean, support everyone here in getting out as well."

The room applauds at José's explanation and John says, "And that right there earned you a point."

There's more applause and the people around José congratulate him. I turn to James. "Is that monitor by the door a tally for each of us?"

"You are quick," he says. "That is your daily reminder of just how close or far away you are from getting out."

John turns back to me. "So, what questions do you have?"

I have so many, like how long does the chip last? Are we tracked after thirty days? Where do we go if we are pulled back in? How many kids have gotten clean and are out past thirty days? But I ask none of these because some part of me tells me not to, makes me think that José will lose the point he just earned, and that part lets me know that this is how the game is played, and this is my first move.

"I'm good," I say.

John smiles, but in it is the eye-twinkle of a man who knows I've been brought into the fold.

I shiver for a moment, realizing how quickly that just went down. It's only day one of being clean, government-style.

8

After group—if you can call it that—we line up again and follow Rashad. "Where are we going?" I ask the kid in front of me.

"We get an hour of free time, now, while another crew goes to group."

"Fuck, yes. I need a break."

We come to a room at the end of the hall and Rashad waves. Someone inside opens the door.

"Hello, Gerry," Rashad says, and Gerry greets everyone as they enter.

"Good morning, Kenny," he says to me. "Are you starting to get a handle on things?"

"Yes, sir," I say, because it makes the most sense, not because it's even close to the truth.

Gerry nods and then verifies that the door is locked behind us. He then sits in a corner and picks up a tablet.

"He's like a babysitter," Devon whispers. "Gerry will read while we're in here, unless we get too rowdy. He's not really necessary with all the cameras and shit. Must be some bullshit government thing."

"What's he do then?"

"Signals to them." Devon looks up and I follow his lead. The ceiling is covered in cameras and microphones.

"And they are?" I ask.

He puts an arm around my shoulder. "Come on. We'll answer all your questions, but we've got to sing first."

I don't bother to question or to argue. I follow Devon to the circle the group has already formed. There's a seat for me on one of the two couches facing each other. The group has filled in behind the couch, so when I sit, I have someone's belly pressed against my head. Including me, there are five white kids of this group of nine. I've met Big James, but not the rest. I know Rashad, Devon, and Ramirez, and I was kind of introduced to José today, so that leaves only three I don't know. Three kids whose lives, apparently depend on mine, and vice versa.

The kids standing start singing. I'm not religious, but it doesn't take much to figure out it's a church song, with all the references to Jesus and

52

whatnot. I look around and Rashad is barely holding in a laugh. He bends at the waist and waves me toward him. We're so close our knees are almost touching. He whispers.

"Don't worry, we ain't gonna try and convert you or nothing. This is the only way we've figured out to speak to each other without Them hearing us. Trust me, we started with rap and that shit got shut down quick. But they're cool with Hymnals, and so we sing above, while we talk below."

This is a massive relief. "Holy shit, thank you. I was starting to bug a little."

"No doubt. When I first got here, I was like, my life is over. I'm some robot in some game or something."

"Exactly!"

"Yeah, don't worry, I fill you in, and then, like we all know how to do, you'll play along and be all right."

"So, do we actually get clean here? Because I'm not gonna lie, I'm jonesing, but not hard. I'm too scared."

Rashad smiles, but it's a slow, sad one. "That's the point man. This place don't care about you. They care about controlling you." He pauses. "But, for real—and I hate to admit it—but something about that does work. I think about H all the time, but then I go to group and think, fuck no! Besides, I'm most likely the next one out the door. It doesn't always go chronological—you know, first in, first out—but usually."

Above us, the group finishes one song, picks another, and then resumes their singing.

"Don't worry," Rashad says, "we'll teach you the songs."

"So, besides group and this free time," I say, "what's the rest of the schedule?"

"It's weird not to be told anything, right? Or to get pamphlets or contracts. This place just does its own thing it seems, but there is some order. I've connected with some of the guys on the other wings and it's the same over there. You just got lucky to be with us."

I'm hoping that's truth, but I don't say anything.

"So, wake up is at 7:00, and then we all go to breakfast together at 7:30. After, it's back to our rooms."

"And you can't leave your room, right?"

"You figured that out. No, you stay put until they tell you otherwise. You can hang out your door, but that's it."

Well, at least I have something to read. I wonder how the rest stay occupied.

"Then, you might go to medical, you might not. If you're like me, you may get to go to the cafeteria for a snack, and to pick up noobs, like we did earlier."

"How do you do that?"

"You earn points, and after a while, you get privileges. But that's just so they can test you." Rashad looks up and then slides a little closer to me. "You get into a fight, you lose all your points. If you don't do what you're told, like throw away your shit and get in line, you lose a point. You refuse to get out of bed and cooperate, you lose half of your points. You see where I'm going with this?"

I nod. "And once someone's outside, someone from your original ten, you lose five points if they get pulled back for using."

Rashad smiles. "You're a quick learner. Were you good in school?"

"What's school?"

He laughs with me, but then reins it in, because the crew is finishing a song. He waits until they pick up another before continuing.

"So, yeah, then we have group and free time. After, you go back to your room, and then we have private sessions or medical, another group, which is less track and talk, and more fear of the arm."

"What's that?" I interrupt.

"Fear of the arm? Easy. They educate you about the cycle of drugs and poverty and violence and how shitty your life becomes if you can't quit."

"Do they show you what it's like to come back?"

Rashad's eyes pop. "Once in a while. If they showed you that shit on the regular, you might get de-sensitized or something."

"That bad?"

He nods. "Think of solitary, and then combine it with—shit I don't know the movie, but someone before told me it's like that—*Clockwork Orange*. You know it?"

"I do." And I consider how it's possible that all of this is happening here, in this building, and all across this country, right now. Can it possibly work?

Or do they intend to just break people who've made shitty choices and have gotten addicted?

"Don't do that, Kenny," Rashad says.

"Do what?"

"Fuck, like I don't know. Get all up in your head. I don't pretend to know what you're thinking about, but I know it can't be good. None of us has a ton of good shit to draw from, so it wouldn't surprise me if you were drowning in some hell hole of thought up there."

"Well, yeah, I was." I pause. "Thanks, lifeguard."

Rashad laughs. "I can barely swim, Kenny. But I'll do what I can to help you navigate this shit."

"Why? Why you helping me? I'm not part of your ten."

"But you kind of are. I'm still here with you, and so if any of you fuck up, I could still pay the price, even though I'm really just waiting on the last two who got released." He leans forward. "Think of me as the captain of this crew. I've been here the longest and have learned the most. Trust me when I say, I got you."

I believe him. I'm not sure if I should, but I'm also not sure if that's just the part of me who never trusts anyone, or it's just a natural response to something like this.

Above, the boys are singing about Jesus saving us and I think of how nice that would be, some guy who sacrifices for, and then saves us, all. But here in this world, I'm looking at my saviors.

***

Before we leave free time, I make sure to ask Rashad the one question I know matters most. "What do I need to do to get out of here the fastest?"

Rashad nods and the guys above me nod. "Yup, the game," Rashad says. "It ain't as simple as be good, offer to help out, talk to others. All those things are right, but can be turned against you." He points at the ceiling. "Remember that they're always watching and listening. Think like them. Give them the show they need, because they need to sell this shit to the public at some point. The program's only been up and running for nine months. Rumor has it they need to deliver this baby to the public, looking beautiful, before there are more lawsuits and shit."

"So is this, are we going to be like reality TV or something?" I ask.

"Maybe, but, if so, with less drama. This shit is supposed to give people hope."

"Hope?" I look around at all the bleakness, the lopsided light, the white and gray paint of everything, the cameras and microphones. "How?"

"Not for us, Kenny. You must remember that. We're pawns in a game, minor characters who they're going to exploit, who they'll use to show they've figured out addiction rehabilitation. Then they'll make a killing. So much money." He whispers the last part and has this wistful look to him, I want to ask how he knows this, and how we could become a profit, but there is no time left. Gerry stands, claps his hands, and the boys all stand at attention. I follow. "Time's up," he says. The door opens and we form a line, which I realize places Rashad in the front because he's got the most points. I take my place in the back and wonder when I'll see the tenth part of this crew.

We file down the hall and split off to our rooms. I lie down on my bed and fall right asleep.

***

"Kenneth. Kenneth. Kenny."

The voice is distant and I can't place it and I have no idea where it's coming from.

"Sleeping Beauty, open your eyes and quit thrashing around on that bed."

I do as I'm told, and standing in my doorway is the nurse who brought me in this morning. "Hey," I say, and sit up.

"All tuckered out, huh?"

I nod and rub my eyes. "It's so much to take in at once."

The nurse laughs. "There's a joke there, but I ain't saying it. However, I am here to take you to medical, so rise and shine."

"What time is it?"

"A little after eleven. You should have enough time for the exam and then we'll head to lunch. I think it's mac n' cheese today."

My stomach growls as if part of the conversation.

"Well, all right, let's get a move on," my nurse says and leads the way.

I follow him off the wing and down yet another hall. Whoever thought to use this old school is brilliant. Even if I could escape, I wouldn't know which way to go. We come to a set of double doors and he uses the pad to get us in.

We enter another wide-open room, with curtains surrounding exam beds. "What was this?" I ask.

"The band practice room. So soundproof no one will hear you scream when they probe." He claps my shoulder and laughs.

I look up and point to the cameras and mics. "No one?"

He doesn't look up with me. "Well, someone caught on quick."

His tone makes me instantly regret saying a word. I have to remember this is *their* game. Being a showoff may not be the best pawn to play. "What can I say, I should have stayed in school. Maybe I'd be riding a scholarship to college."

My nurse laughs. "Maybe. Grab a seat and I'll get you checked in."

I turn to the bank of connected chairs along the back wall and go to one. There are other patients here, but I'm the only one waiting. My nurse goes over to a counter like you'd find at a doctor's office and chats away with the nurse sitting there. I don't think he really had to check me in, so much as he had to check her out.

The ceiling bubbles up above me in a tiered, step-like manner. I tried playing the saxophone when I was in sixth grade, and we'd come down to a room like this and make terrible noise, pretending like we actually knew what we were doing. I guess this ceiling saved the rest of the school from hearing our death knell sound.

"All right, Kenny, let's go."

I stand up and follow my nurse down to one of the curtained off corridors and an exam bed.

"Hop up and take off your sweatshirt. Dr. Williamson is going to take vitals and ask you a couple of questions. Nothing exciting."

"Does this earn me any points?" I ask, once I've removed my sweatshirt.

"It does, actually. Seriously, Kenny, good on you for getting into it. You're going to be all right."

I smile at my play this round, and then the curtain opens and in walks a stern-looking doctor with a tablet in one hand, and some kind of price gun looking thing in the other. She sets the items on the bed next to me and extends her hand. "Hello, Kenny, I'm Doctor Williamson. We've yet to meet."

I shake her hand and it is smooth and dry, the exact opposite of how I feel. She notices and wipes her hand on her lab coat.

"Are you nervous around doctors?"

I nod. It's impossible to have been through as much medical treatment as I have and have formed any other kind of reaction. Docs can make or break you. A friggin' dentist started me down this path.

"Well, don't be," Doc says. "Not around us, at least. We really are here to help you."

I swallow and my throat is super dry. "I'll try," I say.

"Really all we ask, Kenny, is for you to try, and to let us guide you." She picks up the tablet and taps it a couple times. "I just need to run a quick scan of your chip, to make sure it's in place and doing what it should." Doc places the tablet back down and picks up the price gun. "Now, this scan doesn't take very long, Kenny, but it does sting a little. Try to be as still as you can."

"You need me to hold you, Kenny?"

At first I think it's a joke my nurse is making, but when I look at him, his eyes reveal he's serious. Sweat breaks out across my back, because if he's offering to hold me, I think *sting a little* might be an understatement.

While I'm lost in contemplation, Doctor Williamson has already started working. She has placed the handheld device up to my neck and the chip feels like it's vibrating. The sensation runs from my neck to my fingers and toes, up to my head, and swirls around inside. I shudder a bit when it hits my stomach and am truly glad I didn't eat lunch yet or Doc would be wearing it. She gives me the side-eye as I start to double over, but catch myself.

"I'm okay," I say, but the words sound meaningless.

She scans for another thirty seconds. My body vibrates and pinpricks of sensation push in and out. I know the chip is a GPS with other sensors for drugs and such, but it feels as if something else is alive inside. Like I have a jelly fish living in my neck, and its tentacles are trailing everywhere.

Then she's done. The handheld device is lying back on the table and she's scouring the results on her tablet. The sensation lasts, pulsating for another few beats, until it trickles and then stops, dead.

"Kenny, on a scale of one to ten, how much do you want to use?" Doctor Williamson asks.

Henry's words coming out of the doctor's mouth are disconcerting, but I pull myself together and give the question consideration. I've been too busy adapting to think too much about H, but the cravings are still there. Best not to tip my hand, though, just in case. "Weird, but I haven't felt like using at all. So, I guess I'd say a one."

Doc nods. "That's typical, actually. Your body is overwhelmed, but once you settle in, the cravings will come back." She pats my leg. "That's why we're here, to help you with that."

I think of this moment as it might appear, shot through the camera above me, filling a flat screen TV in millions of homes across the country. Rashad might be right, because I have no idea whether or not Doc is being honest with me, but I am positive of what I feel—hope.

9

The cafeteria is packed. Every wing is down here, according to the rest of the guys. The only discernable difference between any of them and us is the color of their sweat suits. They eat and talk and glance up at the surveillance equipment.

"You okay, Kenny?" Big James asks. "Or does your trip to medical have you all scrambled?"

"How do you know I was at medical?"

He's seated across from me and his forehead wrinkles at the question. "Kenny, please. There ain't a damn thing that goes down here that we're not aware of. I saw your points. You must have been a good patient."

I didn't even look at the board. My entire body has felt kind of loose ever since the appointment. All I wanted to do was lie down when I got back. "How many did I get?"

"Five," Rashad answers. "You keep that up. That's the way through."

I want to talk to him about the thought I had while with Doc, about how there's more than just the chip, but I can't get into that now, not with all eyes and ears on us. "Can I ask a question?"

They all turn to me, and I'm momentarily embarrassed to ask.

"Is it about medical stuff, treatment things?" Devon asks. "'Cuz if not, we have to cover that conversation like we do during free time."

"It's about treatment," I say. "But let me know if I go too far."

Everyone nods, so I take the green light.

"So, they asked me about wanting to use. It's weird, I haven't had too many urges yet. Is that normal?"

The guys all nod their heads. Devon speaks. "You're way too out of it at the beginning. Give it a day, you'll see. I'm not hoping that for you, but the cravings return."

I swallow my food and try to will myself not to ask the other question burning inside. I want to build this group's trust, not come off as some paranoid junkie. But I am what I am. "So, while Doc was doing the test, I felt like the chip ran all throughout me. Is that normal, too?"

Now the table goes silent and no one looks at me, except Rashad. "What did they tell you about that?" he asks.

I feel a pit open in my stomach, as if I really have gone too far. "Nothing. I didn't ask. Was too freaked out by the sensation."

He nods and so do the others and the momentary tension seems to have lifted. "Ain't nothing to worry about. That wand they use, whatever frequency that is, just fucks with you. Makes your nerves feel like they're on fire."

Rashad's tone is different, but I don't know if that's just my perception because I'm still getting my feet underneath me, or if what I'm reading is accurate—that he's feeding me an enormous line of shit. Because that's not how I felt at all. Something separate from me, is in me. Or so I think, but realize right now, that whatever it is, I cannot discuss it with them.

"Makes sense," I say. "Thanks." I finish my lunch without another question.

We get word to throw away our garbage, so we do, and line up for whatever's next. I still feel disoriented, but when I see the nurse who brought me to medical, he smiles and says, "Hey, Kenny, what's good?"

I play along. "I don't know? Where am I going now?"

"You got Art therapy now."

"Huh, well, then that's what's good."

He laughs and tells me to have fun and I feel as if I've passed a test. If he thinks I'm good to go, then maybe I am. Or maybe there never was an issue and I'm just paranoid, which is pretty damn typical for me.

We move down the hall, pass our wing, and continue on to another hallway. Once there, we take a left and come to a door. Our nurse waves and the door unlocks. The room must have originally been an art room, because the smells of paint and clay hang heavy in the air. Paint spills on the table carry over onto the floor and years of washed brushes stain the backsplash above the sink. At the front of the room stands a middle-aged woman in a heavy, black apron. Her sleeves are rolled to the elbow and she stands with her hands on her hips.

"Hello, my blue men, and how are we today?" The guys grumble responses and she shakes her head. Then she sees me and makes her way over to my table.

"And you must be Kenny. Nice to meet you. I'm Mrs. Di Angelo."

I shake her outstretched hand. "Nice to meet you," I say. "I've always liked art therapy."

"So, not your first time at the rodeo?" She laughs when she asks.

"No, sadly, it's not."

"Nothing to be sad about, Kenny. You have another shot at life. And most art therapy is the same, so chances are, you'll enjoy this, too." She walks away and claps her hands, gaining the attention of our wing.

"Today, I'd like you to create a portrait. It can be a self-portrait, if you'd like, or of someone you love or hate. But what I want you to think about before you begin is how this person is responsible for your addiction. Show that in his or her face, or in the way they hold themselves. You can use props, but I'd rather feel the answer than be hit over the head with it. All right?"

The group nods and I follow their lead as they grab easels and canvases. Some grab oil paint, others pencils or chalk. I've never liked paint because it's too difficult to work with, not nearly as precise as I like things to be, so I take a canvas and a handful of charcoal pencils and eraser and head back to my table. I set up and then look to see what others are doing. Most are starting, seemingly taking our therapist's advice. She's making her way around the room, having brief, whispered conversations with each patient.

I look up and find the same surveillance equipment as usual. Mrs. Di Angelo finds me looking up.

"They are compelling, but I don't think they'd make for an interesting image."

I look at her. "It's unnerving how much they're recording."

She looks directly at me. "Excellent word choice. It is *unnerving*. But, apparently, necessary. Who in your life has been unnerving but necessary?"

Even though it's a rhetorical question, I go to answer.

Mrs. Di Angelo wags her finger. "No, no. Create your response." She walks away and forces me to stare at my canvas and envision how I'll draw myself.

I scratch at an outline of my head and shoulders. The result could be anyone. But it's a start. Since I've done this before I know how to section the face and provide proportion to the chin and nose and eyes. But the eyes will be last, because they are everything. From what I've gathered in my rehab stints, it doesn't matter what drug you use, seeing yourself while under the influence is a tipping point. You might laugh, you might cry, you might punch the mirror. And it's not because you're on three hits of acid and your face is melting, or you're so drunk that you cannot imagine anyone seeing you as attractive, it's you seeing you for who you are—an addict. We talk a lot about our addicts and how they control us, but that's such a nebulous idea. It's like we're schizophrenic or have multiple-personality disorder or something. Which some of us do, but for those of us who don't, who use because drugs are fun or are an escape or are just what we do because that's all we know now, when you actually see that addict in the mirror, who is you and yet is not totally you, that shit is unnerving.

I'll never forget the first time. I was only drunk, but it's amazing how similar the face is whether I've been baked on pot or shuffling around after lines of H. I stumbled into the bathroom at this party and pissed like a racehorse. It was eighth grade, I think, and this kid's house was massive. The mirror above the sink ran from the ceiling on down, and spanned the width of the double vanity. So, I got a pretty good look at myself. I struggled to stay upright and my clothes were a little disheveled. I smoothed out my hair and re-organized my clothes. But when I came up from the sink after washing my face, that's when I saw it, the whatever all us addicts have lurking in our eyes.

It's the only way I truly know whether I can trust someone. Because if I'm in group and someone's telling me a sob story and that flicker doesn't emerge, then the story is a lie. That person's not an addict. Sure, your life sucks, but don't blame it on addiction, because that ain't it.

When I wiped the water away, I wasn't quite sure what I was seeing. I thought for a moment that maybe there was something wrong with the mirror, but the house was too nice for something to be up; *I* was the problem. So I looked deeper, into the drowning pools of my eyes, and they looked back at me. There I was, thirteen and fucked up, but whomever was looking back was ageless, an old soul, yet also young and reckless. It knew everything and yet nothing. It simply wanted. Needed. Demanded.

It messed me up so much that when I came out people asked me if I was okay. I brushed off their questions and went straight to the keg. But the beer I chugged wasn't enough. I could still see inside my head. My dealer was chilling on the couch. He wasn't yet my dealer, but all it took was for him to look at me, really see my eyes. He handed me a pill then, and for the rest of the night, even though I knew that son-of-a-bitch was lurking, I was able to ignore him. Soon enough, that was all I craved.

Standing before the canvas now, I see those eyes again. I've sketched them just so. The rest of me is only outline.

I must have missed the cue to clean up, because the guys are moving around the room. I reach up to take the canvas down and store it with the rest, but Di Angelo's arm grabs mine. "Hold on," she says. I do as I'm told and stand with her while she examines my drawing.

She nods and nods, but her mouth is tight. Her eyes dart back and forth, and then finally, she looks at me.

"Well done. Those eyes scream, don't they?"

"All the time," I say.

She clasps my shoulder. "Well, I'm glad you recognize that." Mrs. Di Angelo gives a squeeze, and then her hand trails to my neck. She brushes where the chip has been inserted and there's energy in the moment. "Now we'll see if what we've placed inside can finally silence them."

10

I've reached my breaking point for the day. I ask to use the bathroom while the guys are cleaning up and Mrs. Di Angelo lets me go. The stall is like any other school bathroom, except there are no mirrors and there are cameras above the toilets, urinals, and sinks.

I piss and wonder if the staff get together during breaks to watch highlight reels of us trying to sneak one past them, or plotting our demise by toying with shit we can't understand. Like this chip. And whatever else is in me.

I wash my hands and know I have to find out what else has been done. The images they have during group and the knowledge about whether people have used or not, suggest there's a hell of a lot more than some GPS and drug sensing software.

When I get back to the room, someone has put my sketch away and the line is forming. I take my place at the back and Mrs. Di Angelo says, "Nice work, today. We'll continue tomorrow."

A nurse I haven't met before leads us out into the hall. We're silent. More silent than before. I know I have a lot to learn, but some things you don't need to be told. If you're aware of your surroundings, of others, you can feel the message. Right now, it's *shut the fuck up*. The guys keep their heads lowered and shuffle along. I join.

"Lots of messed up shit in there, today," the nurse says, almost to himself. He's a thick-necked, white guy, who reminds me of a lacrosse player, all loose but keyed up.

"I mean, Big James, that portrait you were painting of your mom. Damn! No wonder you so fat." He laughs in that way that assholes do, trying to draw others in, so it seems like the joke is actually funny. No one joins him.

"And Devon, was that your Daddy or your boyfriend. Couldn't tell. Those eyes looked like they were in the bedroom, if you know what I mean." The nurse elbows Devon, who does not look up. I have a feeling if this were the streets things would go very differently.

"This is why pieces of shit like you need this treatment. Sure, if you can change, great. But how likely is that? Once you leave, unless we help you out, you'll all be back doing what you do best." He catches my eye, and I know I should look away, but I can't. "Promise me that the next time, you'll actually OD. Get it right."

His comment may not have been only for me, but it feels that way, as if he's reached into my chest and has squeezed my heart. It beats erratically and I follow the line onto the wing, wondering if I might pass out. "Good night, ladies," the nurse says, just before the door closes behind us.

No one moves. Maybe we're waiting for something. Maybe we're all just too pissed to go forward. Because shit talk like that riles you up, and I bet the others have one way of dealing with it, and that just isn't an option now.

Then a whisper, like the wind blowing through trees, moves from the front of the line to the back. The kid in front of me turns, but only so far that his chin peeks over his shoulder. "Stay strong; sleep tight; get out." He nods toward the points board and all of our totals have gone up. I get it. Technology or not, new program, or some old-school roughing it in the wilderness facility, it all has to be approached the same way—one day at a time.

Then the line moves up the hall and toward our rooms. I repeat the mantra in my head and when I peel off to my room the guys yell, "One day down, Kenny."

I'm floored by the fact that this has only been one day. I'm so exhausted I don't care if they leave the lights on all night. I could sleep with my eyes open.

When I enter, though, I perk right up. Sitting on the edge of the other bed, is an enormous black kid. His eyes are level with mine, and I wonder how that's possible. But in that same instant, I also know who he is. "Mike?"

His face breaks into a smile. "Kenny?"

We clasp hands and he stands to embrace me. On his feet, he's got to be seven-foot. I feel like a child.

"Holy shit!" he says. "How funny is this? Last I heard you, you were pissing liquid gold."

We both laugh and I say, "What about you? How'd it go?"

He sits back on his bed and I move over to mine. "Like they said. Pure torture. I'd been on a bender, so I had so much shit in my system, I think you could have gotten high off my sweat. Took forever to kick."

I think about this, because I was only talking to him this morning. Either he's lying about the amount of drugs he was on, or they pushed it through him somehow. I touch the chip in my neck and ignore his timeline. "You know about this?"

"What?"

"Touch your neck, where I have my hand."

Mike's hand creeps up, and I can see the bulge in his neck before his fingers find it. When he does, he pulls his hand away. "The fuck is that?"

"You know about those chips they put into dogs in case they get lost."

"Sure. But like I've never had a dog."

I cup a hand over my mouth. "Well, it's like one of those, except it has way more information about you on it, and GPS and other shit."

He mimics me cupping my mouth. "Why you talking like this?"

I look up and Mike follows my lead. He sighs and then says, "Shit. They watching."

"And listening."

We sit for a moment, saying nothing. I'm happy for the company, but I don't know if I'll have the energy to answer Mike's questions about everything. I barely know anything, anyway.

"It's just like my boy described," Mike says.

"What do you mean?"

"He was in one of the first wave that got brought in. Got out 'bout a month back. He became like this urban legend, or like that dude in the drawings, Waldo. We all tried looking for his ass, but none of us could find him. That's cuz we was looking in the usual spots. His ass was going back to school and shit."

It's exactly liked they showed at group. "Did you find him? What did he say?"

Mike's eyes go wide. "We found him all right, like a week after he got out. He didn't even know us."

"He brushed you off. Tried to move on?"

"No, man. That would have made sense. Like, he literally didn't recognize us." Mike pauses, looks up and then shrugs. "It took a while, but we showed him pics of us from our phones and the more we talked, the more he remembered. Still, though, it's like he had this block or something."

I'm not surprised. I think the government has a hell of a lot more leeway with us than they're letting on, but I keep that to myself. If Mike wants to run his mouth, that's his business.

"What happened?" I ask.

Mike leans forward, and when he speaks his voice is lower, not quite a whisper, but much more careful. "Someone said he got tased. Somebody else said something went wrong with the metal detector at school. Whatever it was, that chip—" he points at his neck "— that shit got fried. He came 'round with this big ass hole where it was. And the most fucked up part, he was like he used to be."

It takes me a moment, but I ask, "How so? Like personality?"

Mike goes to answer, but then someone shouts, "Lights out in five. If you gotta piss, go now."

A nurse comes to our door and looks at us. "I went during art therapy," I say.

"I'm good," Mike says.

"All right," the nurse says, and then makes a gesture toward the ceiling. The door cranks to life and slides closed. There's a small opening for a window and the nurse says, "Holler if you change your mind," and then is gone.

I stare at the door. I know it's locked, but I also know I could get out by asking. But only to the bathroom. It dawns on my how fully gone my life is.

"You ain't ever been to Juvie, have you?" Mike says.

I shake my head.

"Yeah, I could tell. That door, man. Getting locked in. That's it. That sensation never leaves you."

We sit and listen to guys heading to the bathroom and the clanking of doors shutting. A few minutes later and the lights go out. I look up at the cameras. They have night vision for sure. I can only imagine what they see.

"So, like I was saying," Mike says, but stops. "You want to hear this?"

"Hell, yeah," I say and get under my covers. They're crisp and clean and smell like bleach, but the bed is like lying on the floor it's so hard.

"All right, but it's your nightmare," Mike says. "So my boy is legit his old self. He calls us by our nicknames, shows up at our score spots, starts using again. We were all like, what the fuck, the government's program sucks. Then one day we saw these black cars driving around our neighborhood. They were so outta place it was hysterical. Until it wasn't. Because once they saw my boy, they locked up the brakes and went after him. He ran, but since he'd been using again, his body was for shit. They cuffed him and hauled his ass away. Didn't say a word to us."

"So, what happened? Was it the program? The cops?"

Mike's lying in bed, too, and his voice sounds as tired as I am, but he powers through. "No idea. Lots of people had theories, but the only one that made sense was the program. I mean, that shit in his neck fried, so sure, they probably wanted that fixed. But what we couldn't understand is why that changed him. He told us it was just a tracker. And then—"

I pick up the sentence. "And then there was more to it."

"Isn't there always?" Mike says.

I think about the day, and even test myself, thinking about H, but I feel nothing, no cravings. This chip, this program, all of it, we're only seeing the surface.

"Mike," I say.

It takes him a moment to answer, and when he does it sounds like he's pulling himself out of sleep. "What you thinkin'?"

"You know it only took you a day to kick, right?"

"Yeah, I do. Talking to you cleared that up. I swear it felt longer, though."

"And you don't seem scared. Like, I've been bugging all day, and you're ready to go to bed as soon as I stop talking. Why's that?"

Mike leans on his side. "You never been to Juvie, I have. Dad, uncles, cousins, all locked up. I've visited prison. This shit," he holds up a hand to the room, "this is like a hotel." He says nothing for a moment and then asks, "Where'd they pick you up?"

I'm not sure why it matters, but I answer. "Home. I OD'd." The idea seems so foreign, even as I say it. It's as if it happened to someone else.

"I'm sorry about that, Kenny. For real. Were you trying to, you know, end it?"

"Maybe."

Mike grunts. "I hear you. They found me in a street. Like, just nodded out in the middle of some intersection." He laughs. "It's fucked up. I've been homeless for a year, more, I can't remember. So, I don't know, maybe I'm not scared because this is better than where I've been. Or maybe I'm numb because that's how they want me to be. These chips, how I kicked so fast. My boy. How deep this go?"

He's asking *the* question, and I have no clue how to answer, but possibly Rashad or Devon will. However, I do have one question of my own for him.

"You want to go back?"

"Where? Home?"

I hesitate, but then say, "Yeah."

He smirks. "What's home? I don't even know where my mom lives."

"But when you get clean, you want to get out, right?"

"I'm gonna be straight with you, Kenny. I have no idea. I'ma feel this place out, see how it goes, and then I'll decide."

"But your freedom, your boy?"

"Exactly. I need to find out what they did to him. It might be safer to be in here than to be out there. So..." he doesn't finish.

"So, you're the one in ten," I say and feel like my spine has been hung up on the wall.

"Huh? What's that mean?" Mike says.

"You'll find out. We all will." I roll over and the lights snap off.

11

The lights snap on and there's yelling outside my room. "Rise and shine! It's breakfast time!"

I rub my eyes and feel how dry they are. My mouth as well. It's like I slept all night in a dehumidifier. I'm still wearing the blueberry outfit and with the way it's clinging, I must have been sweating all night. I'm going to stink something fierce.

"Holy fuck, do I gotta piss," Mike says and his voice startles me. I slept so hard it's like I was drugged, and for a moment I thought I was alone.

Mike rolls over and charges to the door, which is still locked. "Hey! Hey, yo! Could you let me out? I don't want to start the day by pissing myself."

The door chugs open and Mike runs out. One of the nurses yells at him to slow down but I doubt he does.

I put my feet on the floor and find my slides. Rubbing my face only makes me feel more tired, so I pray they have coffee at breakfast, even the gritty instant kind.

Mike returns and flops onto his bed. "Holy hell, that felt awesome."

"You are one wide awake motherfucker, aren't you?" I say.

He leans on an elbow. "Annoying as fuck, right? I've always been a morning person. Even if I was out all night, I'd wake up around six and be ready to go."

"Well, we can all be thankful that the government didn't change that."

Mike stands. "Oh, you a snarky one, huh?"

"And you are tall as hell. How big?"

"Bigger than yours, that's for sure."

"Ha, ha. Seriously."

"Last I knew, I'm seven, one."

I whistle at that. "Sports?"

"Please. The only dexterity I have is with a needle. Besides, I never liked all that playground bullshit. Not tough enough, not by a longshot."

I find this hard to believe. Someone that tall would be pressed into playing, whether they wanted to or not.

"What's up, Kenny?" Rashad says from outside the door. "You got a roommate!"

"That's Rashad," I say to Mike. "I'm betting this is the line for breakfast."

Mike goes over to Rashad and looks out the door. "Rashad, I'm Mike. How's this shit work, because I'm ready to eat Kenny I'm so hungry."

"No worries. Order is by arrival. You're the newest, so you're at the back, behind Kenny."

"Shit. Well, get your ass up, Ken, we got food to eat." Mike heads out the door and I follow.

As I pass, Rashad says, "He's a live wire."

"You have no idea."

I take my spot and we move forward. Mike, fortunately, falls silent. We go out the wing and then down to the cafeteria that's filling up with the other wings as well. We claim a table and then get in line.

"So, no guards?" Mike asks.

"No. Nurses. But there are guards. Elsewhere."

"Where?"

"I don't know. The place you go if you fuck up, or if you get pulled back."

I can feel Mike's weight on me. "You mean the place where my boy's at?"

"Yeah, I guess," I say and move up the line, toward the greasy looking eggs and the ladies serving them up. "What's his name by the way?"

Mike doesn't answer at his normal decibel. "Chase."

The serving lady nods to the eggs and I nod back and she scoops a blob onto my tray. "Chase?"

"Yeah, why?"

"Nothing, that's just not what I expected."

"What, you thought like, Tyrone or Jamal or some shit?"

I agree to bacon and sausage and struggle to form an answer. Then I just go with the truth. "Yeah, I did. Sorry. I was just figuring it was a black kid's name."

"You probably figuring he just my friend, too."

Now I turn. "Mike, no disrespect, but I don't know your story. I don't have any caffeine, and I'm starving. So, if you got something to say, go ahead. I'm sorry that I made a dumb assumption."

People are looking at us now, so I wave to the nurses and turn back around. I get some bread and spy the coffee at the end of the serving counter.

"It's cool. I'm just sensitive about it. Chase is my boyfriend, and he's white as Casper."

"How tall is he?"

"What? That's your question?"

"Yup."

"Um, like five, ten or so. Why?"

"I need to see the two of you reunited. He must only come up to your nipples." I look over my shoulder at Mike and he's trying to hold in a smile. I'm glad he's not pissed. "You ever place a drink on his head, you know, like your personal pub table?"

He cracks up now. "Turn your ass around and get that coffee. And yes, I have, and he hates it."

We all join up at the table and Big James marvels at the amount of food on Mike's plate. "You and me are gonna get along, I can tell."

The food isn't half bad and the coffee perks me up, and we eat and Mike gets introduced to everyone, and I feel this weird pang of pride over him, like he's my brother or something, and I'm glad he's making friends. Then he opens his mouth.

"So how you think they do it? Is the chip like wired to our nervous system or some shit?"

Big James puts up his hands. "So, if you want to talk—"

"Fuck that. I know all about the cameras and mics in here. And trust me, they listening to everything. You can't get past it."

"How you know?" Ramirez asks, and because his voice is so low and gravelly, we all turn.

"I had someone go through here, get out, give us the low down, and then get pulled back in."

"What happened?" Devon asks.

"That fucking chip." Mike tells the rest of the story, out loud, not covering his mouth, and the guys look at each other like he's either a prophet or the grim reaper.

When he's done, there's a long pause, and then Rashad asks, "What are you going to do?"

"Find him."

Rashad is staring at Mike as if he's a spider he'd like to kill. The table has gone silent, because they understand, now, what I understood last night—getting Mike to follow the program might prove to be nearly impossible.

"If you had a boy in here, then I'm sure he explained how things work, beyond the technology." Rashad's voice is calm, too calm.

"Yeah, for sure. The whole group of you linked together and shit."

"You mean the group of *us*." Rashad has leaned forward and the veins in his neck bulge. "I have four points to go, and the rest of the guys have been working their asses off to get to the magical one hundred." He pauses, looks toward the nurses and then back at Mike. "So, are you going to fall in line or are you going to be a problem?"

Our nurse smacks his hand on the table. "Well, well, look at you. You've got your ten and now you're telling campfire stories."

We all jump, except for Mike; he seems lost in his own thoughts, in whatever his answer was going to be. Then Big James says, "What do you mean? The campfires I had, we just got wasted and talked shit."

Our nurse shakes his head. "Well, rednecks do that." He looks at Mike and then me. "Some of you seem to be telling ghost stories."

Of course he was listening. We are going to have to get Mike to shut up.

No one answers him and he nods at this. "Group is next. Go get cleaned up."

We bolt from our seats and throw away our garbage, line up, and then are allowed back onto the wing. Once back in our room, Mike says, "Maybe I shouldn't have said anything."

"Probably. And Rashad does have a point. He's practically out the door, and everyone else wants to follow him. So—"

"So I'd better toe the line? Not worry about Chase?"

I feel where he's coming from. In his shoes, this would be a monumental struggle. "You're going to have to figure out how to do both. He needs you, but we also need you. You're hamstrung."

"Hamstrung? The fuck that mean?"

"It's an expression. Like you're being held back from doing what you want." I bend over to get the toiletries from the foot locker.

"Right, 'cuz you all educated and whatnot," Mike says, grabbing his own stuff. "I peeked at that journal. Don't know why you blacked it out, but those are some solid ideas in there."

I stand and see my uncle's journal on my nightstand. "You read that?"

"Sorry. Like I said, morning person."

I'm surprised I'm not angry. "Well, it's not mine. My uncle gave it to me when I got out of my last rehab. It's *his* from the last time, when he succeeded."

"No shit? Why'd he black that shit out? Is it all pervy?"

"No, *they* did that. Whatever he wrote, it doesn't fit with how they want us to think."

Mike nods. "I could see that. You can kind of read between the lines with what he was saying, and it doesn't fit with the robotic vibe we got here."

I move closer to him because I don't want them to hear this part of our conversation, if that's even possible. "So, what's the gist?" I whisper.

He catches on and leans down. "You haven't read it?"

I shake my head, feeling embarrassed now.

"Well, you have to. But, mostly, it's all about being your own person. Work on fighting your addict, and don't be blinded by some program." Mike pauses, then smiles. "Here's a word I know, *irony*. Like what I just said, and what you're asking of me with this crew."

"Yeah, that fits. And so does conformity, because, you are going to have to step in line. There's no way around that one. Unless you want to be like Chase and get redacted."

Mike's eyes flare for a moment, and I fear he might hit me, but then he settles. "I feel you. And I see how this shit could play out if I just say fuck it all to you guys. Then I'm doubly fucked, stuck in here, *and* without Chase." He looks up at me, and his eyes are covered in a sheen of tears. "Help me, Kenny. Please. I know you don't know me, but trust me, I'm no good to anyone if I don't have any hope."

Hope is a word I felt a flicker of yesterday, but before then, I can't even remember. "Mike, man, we're all gonna help each other. That's how this works—"

"That's not what I mean and you know it! You saw how the guys reacted to my story. There's no love there, and there won't be 'cuz they're all worried about their own asses."

"And I'm not?"

Mike wipes his eyes. "No, you are, but it's different, I can tell. Maybe it's 'cuz you just got here, or maybe you're just a different person. Regardless, I feel like we might need each other in here. I got your back if you got mine."

This is not a situation I am prepared for. Mike's asking more of me than anyone has in the longest time. Even in my other rehabs, we depended on each other, but not like this. Which is why I say, "We get clean together. We find Chase together. Then we get the fuck out of here, together."

We shake on it, but then Mike pulls me into a hug. "Thanks, Kenny," he whispers.

We take off to the bathroom, where one of the nurses hands us these toothbrushes that are like straws. They're single use, with the toothpaste already dried on, and are about as sturdy as celery. But they get the job done. Between that and washing my face I feel much better. When I see Rashad, I ask, "So when do we get to shower?"

"Same time we do our laundry."

"Once a week?"

"Yeah, so use that deodorant." He slaps my back and leaves the bathroom, but not before shooting Mike a dirty look.

Five minutes later we're in line and I give Mike the lowdown on group.

He stares at me. "So, one day they must have all gone to group and Chase was what? Offline? What did they say to those guys?"

I don't have a full answer, so I tell him what I'm sure of. "That they just lost five points."

He tilts his head.

"They'll explain it further. But like what I said last night, the one in ten. Yeah, this group, we'll live and die by them."

He looks at me for a long moment and then says, "Or vice versa."

Our nurse brings us through the door and down the hall and then we're at the group room. We walk in and take a seat, but the screen from yesterday isn't on. John, the therapist, is here, with his beady eyes and goatee. He introduces himself to Mike, like he did with me yesterday, and then we all sit.

"Gentleman, since we've had no change outside—everyone's behaving themselves—I figured today would be a good time to work through how you will behave once you get outside." He looks us over for a reaction, but when none comes, he claps his hands. "Okay, let's begin with our mantra."

"Stay clean by any means," everyone says, including me. Mike's eyebrow raises.

John asks, "What if someone slips you a bag?"

The group says, "Stay clean."

"What if a former friend tries to convince you to take 'just one hit'?"

"Any means."

Mike whispers to me, "Is this dude talking about me or am I being paranoid."

I think for a second and then say, "Both."

John asks, "If you use, who are you hurting?"

"All ten," comes the reply.

"Do you want to be that one in ten?"

Mike's head tilts back, like a realization is spreading through it.

"No, sir!"

"Do you remember what happens if you leave here but have to come back?"

"Yes, sir!"

Mike all but snaps in his seat at this. John looks at him. "Yes, Michael? You seem to have a question."

"What does happen? You know, if you come back?"

Instead of answering, John looks around the room. "These boys will tell you. They know. And since you all love to tell so many stories, I'm sure they'll help you out." When John looks back at Mike, his eyes seem to flicker or shift, something disturbed or non-human.

12

After John's cryptic statement to Mike, he launches into a lecture about seeking positive reinforcements when we leave, via a PowerPoint filled with images of former patients out in the real world, enjoying homecoming parties, and going back to school, or starting a job. Either the photographer wanted everyone to look like stock photos, or they actually were stock photos and not real patients, because no one leaving rehab looks that put together. Rashad should be out in a few days at this rate, and even he looks like he could use a week at the beach.

Gerry waves at us as we enter the free-time space and I take the opportunity to go over to Rashad. "I think we should talk. Like *talk.*"

I can't read Rashad's face completely, but it goes from pleased to less than. He signals to the others and Mike and I sit across from him and Devon. The rest of the guys strike up a hymn. Mike looks up at the singing crew but does not ask what's going on.

"You know, Kenny, you seem awfully comfortable awfully fast," Rashad says.

"I agree," I say, "and that's part of the problem, don't you think?"

"What do you mean?" Devon asks.

"You two have been here a while. How long did it take for you to stop jonesing?"

They look at each other and shrug. "Not long," Rashad says. "Why?"

"Don't you think that's strange? I mean, we've all been to other facilities. Something about here sure is different."

"But that's the point," Devon says. "That's why we're doing so well. This program actually works. You've seen the guys outside and how they're succeeding."

I wait for Mike to counter that, but he doesn't. "What about the ones who don't succeed?"

The guys finish a song and there's a lull while they pick another. However, even if they were still singing, I think Rashad would be giving me the same pissed off look he is now. He's not angry that he has to wait, he's pissed at the question.

The guys sing and Rashad leans forward with his elbows on his knees. "I need four more points to get the fuck out of here. Probably three by the end of the day, so, what, exactly, are you trying to say, because I really don't have an interest in listening."

No wonder Mike's staying quiet. He must have sensed this is where we were going.

"Mike's friend," I say, and Mike doesn't look at me, just stares ahead. "Well, he was here, and then out, and then the chip in his neck fried, and they pulled him back in."

Devon looks at Mike. "That true?"

Mike nods. "He didn't come back."

Rashad's face looks slick with sweat. "What do you mean?"

"Like I just said." Mike's angry now. "I know you don't want to hear this shit. The light at the end of the tunnel is waiting for you, but what light is it, huh? When you leave here you won't be the same. Sure, you won't want to use, which is a win, but I'm telling you, once you're out these doors, you'll be a fucking zombie."

"And I'm supposed to believe this, because you know *one* guy?"

Mike stares Rashad down. "No. You should believe me because the person I loved and who loved me back didn't even recognize me when he got out."

I let that sink in for a second and then say, "You heard John tell Mike that you all know what happens to people when they get pulled back. So, what is it? What happens?"

"If what you're saying about your boy is for real, then you don't want to hear this, Mike," Devon says.

"But I do. I want the truth."

Rashad starts laughing. It's a little pop that soon takes over the room. The boys stop singing and Rashad's laughter echoes around us.

"Truth?" Rashad asks. "No, you want to hear some sweet story about how he's being taken care of. I can't tell you that."

"Why's that?" I ask.

Rashad looks from Mike to me. "Why you getting into this Kenny? This isn't your problem. Yesterday you were falling in line, figuring this out. Today you're demanding answers about shit that don't concern you."

"How doesn't it concern me? What if the same shit happens to me? What if I use when I get out?"

"You won't."

"How do you know that?"

"Because if you do, you'll die."

Devon elbows Rashad. "Shut up!"

Rashad shakes his head. "No. I'm putting this shit to bed right now. I'm not having these two go off the rails and fuck me over. Best they learn now and toe the line. For the rest of you all, too."

The quiet that falls over the room is more than just the fact that the boys stopped singing. I'm sure everyone wants to hear what Rashad apparently knows, but Gerry's standing and the door is sliding open. In walks Tom Hobson, director of the ward.

He's smiling, completely unbothered by the tension in the room, and walks over to us. "Guys, hey, let's relax. Okay?"

Both Rashad and Mike look equally confused, but the anger still simmers between them.

Hobson walks to their side and slips a hand around their necks. "Okay, let's just take it easy." As he speaks, he presses their necks, and both sit back in their seats, limp. Hobson watches them for a second and then turns to us. "Does anybody else need help relaxing?"

We all shake our heads. I take a closer look at Mike and see that there's nothing going on inside. It's like he's nodded off. Same for Rashad.

"Yes, Kenny, it is like they've been deactivated," Hobson says to me.

I look up, my heart hammering in my throat, wondering how Hobson knew that.

He stands, feet spread apart, and claps his left wrist with his right hand. "Most of you have heard this before—not that you *know* this—so don't worry if it echoes a bit. However, it seems that Mike and Kenny could use to hear it right now." He smiles at me and it feels like he's wielding a scalpel.

"We've been listening. We are always watching and listening. Even through the singing. He laughs at this. "It's our job to monitor you, to make sure that all of your hardware is synching up to your software."

I swallow and feel the chip bobbing against my throat.

"Make no mistake, we are trying to control you. As addicts, you are an absolute drain on our society. We have nothing to lose by experimenting on you. The rate of recovery for heroin addicts is ridiculously small and your population is swelling. Simply, drastic times call for drastic measures."

The guys are staring like they might be watching television, or a game. I hope I don't look as transfixed as them, but maybe I do, because what I'm hearing is fucking absurd. I'm sure my brain can't process this.

"You are part of an experiment. The early patients, with some exceptions, have exceeded our expectations, and so we have the green light to continue. The goal is to expand our work to so many others. Addicts, the mentally disabled, the dissenters in our society. We will function at a much greater capacity with your various scourges wiped away. Especially if you have one goal in mind: to be a good citizen." Hobson pauses and looks directly at me. "You're probably wondering why I'm telling you this. It's because it's for your own good. The technology you have is phenomenal, but it takes time to work and needs encouragement. The human brain and free will and addiction are not easy to parse out. So, we're helping you with that."

Hobson raises his hands to the room. "For all of you, that means living here under our surveillance and being bound to the others. We need to watch you and we need to make you care. You still have to *want* to be better."

Hobson moves closer to Mike and then puts his hands on his shoulders. Mike doesn't move, doesn't seem to realize anyone's touching him, let alone this asshole.

"Take Mike's boyfriend, for example. Chase was doing fine, ignoring Mike and the other kids he used to party with. Then this idiot had to go and use a magnet on his chip, completely disrupting the system." Hobson frowns at Mike like he's a puppy that's shit on the rug. Then he looks up and says, "However, we did learn the electromagnetic threshold from that, so kudos to Mike for helping us out."

Hobson steps away. "And we did bring Chase in, and we almost have him recommissioned. Almost." The way he says this feels like *almost* is one hell of an undefined amount of time.

"It was a tough blow to Chase's group, but they rebounded and have moved forward. Therefore, if you follow the program, you will never have to come back. Your doctor will maintain your system and you will never know the difference."

Hobson stands again with his hand clasped over his wrist, smiling over us like we're a room of students, and he is a titan of a teacher. The guys still look glazed over, so I speak. "How can you do this? What happened to our rights?"

"For those of you under eighteen, your parents signed them over to us. The rest, they signed."

"How is that possible? No one would willingly do that."

Hobson tilts his head at me. "Well, that's some faulty thinking. You have a sense of how many people we have here."

"I do, and it's a lot, and there are centers like this all over the country?" The breadth of this is staggering.

Hobson laughs, clasps and unclasps his wrist. "My you have a lot of questions. Too bad you got into drugs, I bet you would have had a bright future. But to your question, yes. And there will be more. Success brings money."

Me, the real me, I hope, feels a sinking sensation. My future cannot be predetermined like this, by some government experiment, with me as a pawn to make others money.

"But it's not a success, not if you have situations like with Chase," I say.

"Outliers," Hobson replies. "They occur in all experiments. Fortunately, in this one, they can still be reined in." He moves from his spot to the couches where the guys are either sitting or leaning, faces expressionless, and grips their necks. They go from slack to completely blank for a second, and then back to slack.

"And now you can move on with your treatment and this will be a vague memory." Hobson puts his hand to his chin. "More like a dream that's remembered, but not given much thought." The pads of his fingertips glint and then I watch him slip them around Big James's neck. He moves on to the next kid and I see that he's slipping his fingertips over the chips. Just like the handheld Dr. Williamson used.

In a moment he will be to me and there's nothing I can do. The chip's embedded, settling deeper by the day, and by the time I'm out of here it will control me. *That's* what Rashad was trying to say. I will not be cured. I will still be an addict, but I won't feel it. Does that mean I'm no longer addicted? Does that mean I'll even be myself? One of ten.

"Relax, Kenny, this won't hurt a bit," Hobson says and slips his fingers around my neck.

13

I wake up, in bed, with the soft glow of the nighttime lights on in the wing. I roll to my side and Mike's asleep in his bed. And then it comes back to me. The conversation, Hobson, him touching our necks. I feel my own, the chip there, doing whatever it's supposed to. And yet, I wonder. Was that a dream? Because it seemed like it happened this morning and now it's clearly night. What went down between then and now?

The floor is cold against my bare feet, but I don't bother to find my sandals. I scurry over to Mike's bed and sit next to it. "Mike," I whisper. He doesn't move.

I shake his shoulder and say his name again, still nothing. I flick his nose, hard, and that does it. He reaches up to his face and mumbles, "What the fuck?"

"Mike, it's me. Wake up, we need to talk."

Mike rubs his face and then his eyes open and he looks around the room, takes in the darkness and then turns and finds me at his side. "Kenny, what the hell is going on?"

"I'm kind of freaked out about today," I whisper, even though I'm sure the surveillance equipment is picking up this conversation right now.

"What are you talking about?" Mike shifts to his side.

I move closer and whisper even lower. "This morning. You know, after group, and Hobson came in and said all that shit, and then it was lights out for us."

Mike's breath doesn't catch with memory. He doesn't pop up from the bed because of the realization of what I've said. He's as blank as the bedsheet. "Motherfucker, are you sleepwalking or some shit?"

My mind races. I can feel it desperately searching to figure out who's the messed up one in this situation, Mike or my memory. But I remember. It wasn't some dream that I'm now rehashing in my sleep. Not like Hobson said it would be. I know what happened, what is happening. And when I look at Mike, it seems as if I might be alone.

"Seriously, you don't remember anything he said?"

"Who?" Mike asks.

"Hobson!"

"Kenny, I don't know who the fuck you're talking about. Do you need me to get a nurse or something? I think you're starting to crack up."

I slide down onto the floor, doubting my sanity. Maybe I did dream it. How the hell will I know?

"Mike, what did we do today? Like after breakfast."

"Free time. Medical. Lunch. One-on-one therapy. Another group. Dinner. Bed."

That's the day, but I can't remember any of it. "Shit. Why don't I remember any of that?"

"Seriously, Kenny, are you all right?"

I look up at him. He's back-lit by the moon out our window, and his face is wrinkled in sincere worry.

"No, I don't think either of us are. Not if I you can't remember the morning and I can't remember the afternoon."

"Remember what?" he says.

I run a hand through my hair. This conversation could go on for hours and we wouldn't get anywhere. I'm sure whoever's watching it is loving it, though. But then I hit on an idea. I turn to Mike. "Where's Chase?"

"He's...he's..." Mike pauses. "He's here, isn't he? How do I know that?"

"Well, you came in guessing it, but this morning, Hobson confirmed it."

Mike looks away. "Hobson. He's the guy who runs the ward, right?"

"Yeah, he is."

"Creepy looking motherfucker?"

"See, I knew you'd remember."

Mike smiles. "No, I don't, but if he runs a place like this he has to be."

We both laugh, as screwed up as this all is, and then Mike looks up at the surveillance. He scrambles off the bed and grabs my uncle's journal. He opens it and scours the pages. After a moment he jolts and points at a word—*We*. He looks at me and then points between us. I get it and nod.

He returns to his scouring and points at the word *must*. Again, I nod, and then Mike goes back to looking. He repeats the process with the words *challenge* and *everything*.

I find a question mark and tap that until he understands that I need some clarification. Then I find the words *why* and *how*.

Now Mike nods and flips pages until he comes up with the next three words: *know, the, truth*.

The next question I need to ask is going to be difficult, because my uncle most likely didn't write about a guy named Chase, so I scour for a bit and then piece together: *your, lost, love, where* and make sure to tap on a question mark a dozen times.

Mike nods his head vehemently and there are tears in his eyes. He takes the journal from me and although it takes him a few minutes, he comes up with *see, if, your, memory, correct*.

I nod and my eyes drift down to the page open on Mike's lap. I see the question I want to ask written in my uncle's looping handwriting. And so I circle it, repeatedly: *And then what?*

* **

I don't fall back asleep. I stay awake the rest of the night, thinking through all of what I'm in, and what lies before us. I have no idea how much time we're going to have with an ability to think our own thoughts. How far and how quickly does this chip run things? I'd ask one of the guys, but I'm afraid they'll turn me in to Hobson or John or any one of the nurses. Probably get points for that. I guess this is how they keep you in line while you're in here, they keep you from questioning anything so that you conform. Trading one slavish existence for another. Well played government, well played.

At least I have Mike. Because if this were just me, I'd think I was paranoid and would probably let them do whatever they needed so I didn't feel this way. But he's here with a purpose, one he hasn't forgotten—to find Chase. And he's here, somewhere. If we can find him, if we can get some truth, maybe we can warn others. But is that enough? It sure as hell won't save us. But maybe we were never meant to be saved.

The sun brightens the quad outside, and I watch the light climb up the wall. I haven't watched a sunrise while sober in forever. I smile, because it's still beautiful. The world still can be. I am clean. I'm not jonesing. I'm not sick. There is something positive here, but we've got to cut the rest away. I don't believe anyone would want to watch a lifetime of artificial sunrises. The good with the bad, the person with the addict. I can get sober without losing it all.

The nurse yells outside our door, "Rise and shine!" and the door unlocks and slides open. I stretch as if I've just woken up and hear Mike turning on his bed. My joints hurt and my head feels like a clogged toilet.

"Morning, Kenny," Mike says and slides to a sitting position.

"Mornin'," I say and mirror him. I wait. I want to see if he remembers. I know I dreamt nothing because I didn't sleep, but I don't know where he'll be. "You all right?"

He looks up and his eyes are haunted. He grabs my uncle's journal, flips a couple pages and then points at two words: *for now.*

I nod. He nods. We're good, on the same page. "Exactly," I say. "I need some fucking coffee."

"Coffee would be fan-fucking-tastic." Mike stands and I follow him to the bathroom.

Breakfast is fine. Everyone eats and drinks coffee and looks like they've slept like young kids who've played all day. I blend well, but I test the waters, just to be sure.

"Hey, I forgot, did anything go down in group yesterday?"

Heads turn to each other, and pretty much everybody shrugs. "I don't think so. It was as boring as usual." Rashad laughs and most of the table joins him.

My appetite is non-existent, and I know if I force myself to eat, it's just going to come back up, and that will mean a trip to Medical, and who knows what will happen then.

"You think you're going to get that last point today?" Devon asks Rashad.

"Maybe. All depends if fate looks kindly down upon me." He pauses. "And if no one out there blows up my spot."

The table laughs again, including Mike, and I feel so lost. I know Rashad said he needed four, maybe three, more points, not one.

"When did you get those points?" I ask.

Rashad tilts his head at me and squints. "Are you for real?"

I don't have an answer so I just look back down at my plate.

"Kenny," Mike says, "you were the one responsible. Remember? You needed help completing the activity in group and Rashad hooked you up."

It's fortunate that I've spent so much of the past few years unconscious. I've had too many of these moments, where my parents would start with *Remember...* And I never could, but lying was easy.

I shake my head in an exaggerated manner and then put a palm to my forehead. I toss a smile. "Must be how great I slept last night. I completely forgot."

"No shit! I slept so hard last night," Big James says.

The rest of the guys chime in with how well they slept, too, and my blunder seems to have been forgotten.

But then Rashad clears his throat, loud, like a teacher or a minister, someone demanding attention. The entire table turns to him. "Unless you didn't forget. Maybe you're playing us to see what's what?"

A chill runs through me. It's not so much Rashad's challenge, but the look in his eyes, something in between human and not. "What do you mean?" I manage to sputter out.

"You know exactly what I mean. I haven't gotten this far without figuring my way through this system."

Ramirez edges past Rashad's anger to say, "Careful."

We all know what he means, but Rashad and I both seem to know all the singing hasn't mattered. They can cut through anything.

"I am being careful," Rashad says. "I'm watching out for the rest of you. Without you I wouldn't be this close to getting out, but I'm afraid these two are going to fuck you over."

It's like we're picking up where we left off yesterday, but there's no way that's possible, and there's no way Rashad can know the journal-conversation Mike and I had. Unless he does. Unless he's been told. Unless he's being played, too.

"The only one about to get fucked over here is you," I say. "Keep it up and we're throwing down. I've got only a few points to lose. You, you've got everything to lose."

The guys whisper to keep it cool, to chill out. I eye Mike for a second and he has a tight-lipped smile on his face.

"It ain't like that." Rashad stands, gripping his plate like it's a frisbee. "I'm keeping you in line, making sure you follow the program."

I stand as well. "Are you, though? Seems like you want to throw that plate at my face. Pretty damn sure if you do, you can say *see ya* to half your points." I move out from behind the table. Mike gets up and stands next to me. "Also seems like it's not you who's doing this. You still in there, Rashad?"

Rashad's arm shakes. He grimaces at me, seeming to fight not only with his body but his mind. And then a decision is made, either by him or whatever's running the show, because he smashes the plate on the table and the shards fly around us.

"Fuck you, Kenny! You think you know. You think Mike is the only one here who had someone on the outside. I did, too, and he was totally fucked up, a complete fucking zombie. And do you know what happened to him?"

I am sure I know, but it's more important I stay quiet and let Rashad get this out.

"It's like I told you, this fucking thing," he says, pointing to his neck, "it'll fucking kill you if you use." Rashad takes a deep breath, and behind him figures move, not nurses, not Hobson, either.

Before he can say another word, they're on us. Rashad, Mike, and I are slammed to the floor. Our arms are wrenched behind our backs, and zip ties lace our wrists to themselves. Then we are hoisted up, and I can see who's doing what. Guards in all black have taken control of us, just as Hobson enters the room.

They drag us away from the cafeteria, and out the doors, but not before I hear the director say, "Now, everyone, let's take it easy."

Doors open and soon enough we're at the end of a hall I don't recognize. An elevator opens and we get in. The guards pin the three of us behind them, but I turn to see Mike and Rashad both. Mike looks like he's ready for a fight, for whatever's coming at him. Rashad looks like he just lost a battle, and maybe he has.

No one presses a button, but the door closes and we descend. My heart pounds and my entire body throbs with fear, but I remember what Rashad said. I remember Chase. This cannot be the end.

The elevator stops and the doors open to another hallway, this one dark with only scant illumination from overhead lights. We're in the basement. Or deeper. The air is dank, wet almost, and there is no noise aside from our foot-steps as we're marched along.

We enter a wing, like upstairs, but also not like it at all. The doors are all closed, and none have windows. Everything is dark gray and metal. The cold has already seeped into my bones and I shiver. The guard stops before a door and it slides open with a clank. In goes Rashad, and the door slides shut.

Another door opens and Mike's guard prepares to launch him. Mike screams to me, "Stay strong, Kenny!" He is then tossed inside and sealed up.

I don't know how to stay strong, never have. And yet, I know I have to, that we have to get through whatever they're about to do to us, and somehow maintain a sense of who we are. Hobson said parsing out free will and addiction is difficult. Maybe because you can't override a soul.

I'm tossed inside, and hit my head on the wall that can't be more than three feet from the door. I slide to the ground as the door closes. Stars pop in my vision, but dissipate quickly, and when they do there is no light. It's claustrophobic, but I feel around for a bed and don't find one. The only thing in the room, which is roughly the size of a broom closet, is me. Because I am now a thing, for sure. But that's nothing new. Here's hoping that what I can do, is.

14

When I shot heroin, I loved the dark, because it set the stage like a ritual: dimmed lights, a tourniquet, a spoon, a syringe, and my love. It was downright romantic.

Now, the dark has held me hostage. Time is gone. I may have been here for hours, possibly a day. My self-awareness is gone. There's the hard ground, the walls around me, but where I end and the damp concrete begins is a mystery.

Yet, I keep clinging to what I know, what I've figured out from Rashad's and Hobson's comments. There's a chip in my neck—really something much larger than that, a web of hardware—that's designed to control me by first keeping me from feeling withdrawal, and then destroying my desire for heroin, and finally, keeping me subdued, in line.

And yet, there's so much I don't know. Like how Rashad and Devon and Ramirez and Big James were at first so willing to show me the ropes, let me in on the secrets they knew. Then Mike showed up with his knowledge, and some kind of flip got switched on Rashad, and whatever he was supposed to do went to war with who he is. And now all three of us are here, awaiting what?

They're not going to take out the chip. Because if what Dr. Williamson said is true, then once it's settled into you, they can control you. That's why Rashad's the pawn. He's been here long enough for that shit to be steering the ship, if they want it to. No wonder he greeted me when I got here. You need a storyteller to fill in the blanks. You need the audience to buy the lie.

I grab my neck and feel around the hardware inside. There's no heat, nothing to indicate it might blow, but it's also only hard at the very tip. Beneath, or around, I can't tell, is squishy, like the stress balls so many therapists have asked me to use. I swallow and feel it shift away from my neck, but then slide right back into place.

The door clangs, slides open, and I spill out. The dim light hurts my eyes and I claw at them, trying to shield and see at the same time.

"Sit up," the guard's voice says, and I feel his boot under my elbow.

I use it to push myself up and sit with my back against my cell. My eyes are adjusting, and my lungs are sucking up the clean air, but I'm not sure if where I am is any better than where I was.

"Okay, okay, let me have a look." Dr. Williamson's voice is distinct and pushes between the two of us as she crouches down in front of me. She shines a pen light and checks my eyes. Then she has me open my mouth and looks in. She feels around my neck, and I want to say something about the shifting nature of whatever's in me, but realize that would be stupid. Chances are she's the one who implanted the thing.

"So, Kenny, how are you?"

"I've been better, but I've been worse, too, so—"

Doc smiles at this. "Sounds accurate. Well, you'll be happy to know that this procedure won't take long, and we'll have you back up to the ward in no time."

"Okay. How's Mike?"

Doc frowns. "About the same as you. But, don't worry, you and he will have a chance to talk. Actually, if you can get up, we'll bring you to him."

This sounds like a lie, like a total bullshit trap. I've had people screw me over so many times in scenarios just like this. It's always *trust me, Kenny*, and that's when I should have done the opposite. But I don't have much choice here, and if Doc's not lying, I'd like to see Mike before whatever the procedure is.

I rock to my side, get my legs underneath me, and push my way up, with my back to the wall. The guard is watching me the entire time, as if I might suddenly jump him. Once I'm standing, I'm dizzy, but I close my eyes until it passes and say, "All right, let's do this."

"Follow me," Doc says.

We walk down the hall, Doc leading and the guard behind me. The only sound is her shoes clacking. This basement is desolate, and I'm confused about where this procedure will be performed until I see a room up ahead. It's a surgical suite, complete with a bed, and lights, and an entire wall of instruments. Mike's sitting on the bed staring at his feet. "Mike!" I yell and his head pops up.

"Keep it down," the guard says.

I ignore him and pick up the pace and soon pass Doc and enter the surgical suite. I clasp hands with Mike and he looks how I feel, scared shitless. But we laugh and I hop up on the bed next to him. "Have you seen Rashad?" he asks.

"No. You?"

"No, and she said something about a procedure. Kenny, are we fucked?"

"We were already fucked, Mike. How much worse can it get?"

"We're good, Steve. You can head back up. This will take a while, anyway. I'll call for you," Doc says.

The guard asks if Doc's sure, but his tone his obvious—he doesn't give a shit. He walks away and a moment later the sound of some faraway door opens and then closes.

"Gentleman," Doc says, and then leans against the counter across from us. "I'm sure you have a dozen questions, and I will answer them, but first, let me explain what's going to happen to you."

Mike's breathing has gone shallow, and I can feel my heart working double time, trying to process this fear.

"You can forget whatever you were considering about getting to the bottom of things, about finding out the truth. It's really very simple," Doc says.

"It isn't about treating addiction," I say. "It's about controlling us, remaking society."

Doc Williamson smirks. "Well, Kenny, you make it sound so dismal."

"It is, though, isn't it?" Mike says.

"I guess we're skipping to the questions, so okay, here's one, how? You will be better people. You'll have the focus to go to school, hold down a job, get married, and have kids. What's wrong with any of those things?"

"Nothing is wrong with any of that, except it wouldn't really be us doing those things, would it?" I ask.

Doc ponders this. "Technically, sure. But you have to understand that only curing your addiction won't necessarily make you a more productive member of society. You'll have the root of your addiction still embedded within you, with its ability to sprout again, given the right conditions. Both of you have been through numerous centers, and none have worked."

She's right, but still. "So, instead, we're better off with the root of *this* thing," I say, grabbing my neck.

"I'd say you are. So do a lot of policy makers. You know, the people in society who do the work of keeping this country up and running."

"Unlike us," I say.

"Unlike you, yes."

I look over at Mike and wonder how in the hell he got to the point where he ended up here. What's his full story? How'd he become a drain on society, like me, as opposed to something else?

"So what are you going to do to us, Doc?"

She grips the counter behind her. "Emotions are near-to-impossible to control, even with this technology. It needs to settle in, to learn you, to understand what is necessary to keep you from acting on impulse, from flying into a rage, to using again. This all takes time. The chip is the brain, but it's encapsulated with a substance that behaves like neurons. That substance grows off your blood supply and gets to work. It attaches to the major organs, like a secondary nervous system, and once fully formed, links your brain up to our system."

The analogy of the jelly fish I had before wasn't really that farfetched.

"So, we are truly cyborgs."

"Yes and no. You have free will, to a degree. A cyborg is only a program. A.I., yes, but still programmed. There are parameters. Your parameters are more flexible."

"But you can narrow or widen them, can't you?"

"That's a good way of putting it. Yes, once you are completely integrated. And that leads to what I'm doing today." She picks up a scalpel and then with tweezers, holds up a microchip. "The process is taking too long. It leaves us with patients like Rashad, who are ready to go, but would benefit from being released sooner."

"Where is Rashad?" I ask, cutting off Doc.

"Let me finish." She holds out the chip to us. "You need the 2.0 version, which is this. We estimate that we can have you out within one month with this system. You will conform easier, fall into line faster, and not question the system in place. The chip will override your memories from your time already here, and it will be like you've just detoxed and are new on the ward."

"But won't the rest of the guys remember us?"

"No. They will be fitted with the new chips before you see them. Every-one will be new to one another."

"Even Rashad?" Mike asks.

"Rashad has been released," Doc says. "It was time. He has a new chip and won't remember anything from here. It's better that way."

I can't imagine how that is. I don't understand how turning us into cy-borgs is helpful in the long run, for us, or for anyone else. But this is so out of my hands.

"Doc, why are you telling us any of this if we won't remember, if it won't matter?"

"Well, I could be wrong about you remembering nothing, and so I want you to have some sense that we are not—the government—is not some in-humane entity. We do care." She pauses. "Because if we didn't, why would we supply you with such an excellent match for Rashad's replacement?"

Mike and I look at each other, and it's clear that neither of us have fol-lowed the conversation to wherever she's brought it. Doc stands and crosses the hall to another room, not a cell, and not a surgical suite, but what looks like an examination room. She opens the door and out walks a lily-white boy with a starburst scar on his neck.

"Chase," Mike says, and the word sounds like a prayer. He jumps from the table and into the hall.

Chase looks up and sees Mike and his face cracks into a smile. When they hug they both cry, and as I imagined, Chase only comes up to Mike's nipples.

I turn away, to give them a moment, and look at the wall of monitors on the far side of the room. It's the wards, with shifting views from the security cameras. I move over to the monitors and find our ward. They're in Art ther-apy, working on the unnerving images. I tap the screen and a volume icon appears. I press it and the surgical room is filled with the sound of the Art room.

"Excellent boys," Mrs. DiAngelo says. "Don't be afraid to fine-tune those edges, really make what you see in your mind come alive."

"Kenny!" Doc Williamson yells at me.

"Sorry," I say, and mute the image, but as I do, something else catches my eye. There's what looks like a film crew coming in through the patient en-trance. It looks like they're shooting, too. There are multiple cameras, and a boom mic, and some guy with nice hair, who's dressed well, seeming to lead the way.

Doc stands next to me and watches them. I wait for her to yell at me, but she doesn't. Instead, she sighs. "Hobson was supposed to tell us before they showed up."

"Who are they?"

"Filmmakers."

"What are they filming?"

Doc pauses, then taps the screen for the intake bay. She opens up the volume like I did, and the film crew comes to life. "As you can see," the guy with the nice hair is saying, "the patients are treated well, but not pampered." The camera crew seems to focus on a handful of patients lying on beds, detoxing. "Your tax dollars are at work fixing the problem, not merely putting a band-aid on it."

Doc kills the volume and turns to me. "A behind-the-scenes look."

I wonder how much they're going to let the crew film. Medical? Therapy? Are they going to interview patients? "Why are they doing this?"

"Transparency," Doc says. "As patients, you don't have any contact with your families or friends until you leave here. For most that's only a few months. However, some have been here for the nine months we've been up and running. People want to know what's going on."

I look over my shoulder and see Chase and Mike still holding each other, whispering softly.

"The tech or the free will? Which is the problem?"

"I'm hoping it's the tech, Kenny. We all are, even you."

In a way, she's right. I am hoping this fixes things, just not the way they're doing it. If this stupid chip could just stop the addiction, I'd be all in, but since it does so much more, how can I agree to that? Because I won't be me after we're through.

"I'm going to get prepped, Kenny." Doc leaves me, and I stare at the screens. There's so much going on at this facility, so many lives being set on this path. And we're just one operation, at the very beginning. If this is successful, the implications are never-ending.

"Kenny, I'd like you to meet Chase."

I turn and Mike and Chase are holding hands and smiling. "Chase, I've heard a lot about you. It's good to meet you, even though I'm about to forget who the hell you are." I laugh but see both Chase and Mike wince.

"What are you talking about?" Chase says, and his voice is like a life-time smoker's, deep, and crazy raspy.

My heart sinks. I figured he at least knew, and was telling Mike. Fuck. I look at Mike. "We're getting new chips, starting over." I look at Chase now. "All of us. We won't remember the ward from before. They're refitting the other guys, too, and they won't remember us, either."

"How far back are they killing our memory?" Chase asks. "I've barely got any now."

I so want to ask him what the hell has happened to him, but there's no time. Doc's scrubbed up and has arranged syringes and chips and scalpels.

Before I can tell him that I don't know, Mike presses closer, his voice a rough whisper. "Kenny, there's got to be another way. I can't lose him again."

"But you won't. He's our ten. Rashad's out and Chase will round out our group."

"Until they change the rules again, upgrade to a new chip."

I don't know what to say, because he's got a solid point. I turn to the monitors. "They want us out faster, though. They even have a crew filming about what's going on in here. The people have questions."

They look along with me at the wall of monitors. "Where's the elevator to here?" Chase asks.

I look until I find it, but also remember the door that the guard went out. I find the top of the stairwell that the staff must use. There's a door to the outside, there.

"Okay, boys. Time to get down to it," Doc says behind us.

Chase and Mike turn, but I keep my eyes on the monitors, especially the one at the top of those stairs.

"I'll inject a sedative, and when you wake it will be dinner time, and you'll feel brand new. Who wants to go first?"

The film crew has reached the hall above us, and look like they're taking a break. The guy with the good hair keeps tapping his pocket and looking toward the end of the hall. I hope he never plays poker. I turn around. "I'll go first."

A tension seems to drop when I say this, and Mike looks at me, quizzically. I look directly at him. "If this doesn't work, I'm sorry."

Before he can ask what I mean, I hop up on the surgical table.

Doc comes over with an alcohol pad and tourniquet. She checks my veins. "Not bad. Some scarring, but at least they're usable." She wipes down the crook up my arm, tightens the tourniquet, and picks up the syringe. "It's brave of you to go first. Thank you."

"You're welcome. I want to give them as much time together." I look over at Chase and Mike, hoping she'll do the same.

When she does, I move on instinct, grabbing the syringe in one fluid motion and eyeing her jugular at the same time. Doc gasps, but it's too late. I hit my mark, as I've done on myself, and countless others who've asked me to inject them for the first time. I push the plunger, because there's no time to check to see if I've hit the vein. Doc grabs my wrist, but her eyes go slack, and in a moment, she's heavy beneath me. I lay her on the bed.

15

"Mike, grab her feet."

He runs over and helps me situate Doc onto the bed. She looks like she's either sleeping or has nodded off.

"What the fuck, Kenny?" Mike says.

I ignore him and return to the monitors. Sure as shit, the good-hair man is taking a smoke break. He's got the door propped so he can talk to the crew, who seem to be trying to ignore him, while they check their equipment.

"There's our window," I say.

Mike and Chase have followed me to the monitors. "Our window for what?" Mike asks.

"Escape, honey. What else?" Chase taps the screen. It zooms. "That'll bring us out to the parking lot, and from there, we'll be on Division Street. We can make it work."

"How?" Mike asks. "These chips haven't been deactivated. They'll find us. It'll never work." He turns to me. "I meant there has to be another way to not forget. The guys. What about them?"

I can't have Mike losing his shit right now. Yes, this was a split-second decision, but I know it's the right one. We have to get out, first. After, I don't know.

"It's like being a lifeguard," Chase says. "Which, in a former life, I was. You save yourself first before you can save anyone else. We'll get them, honey. Kenny promises." He looks at me and in his eyes I can see that we're on the same page.

"I abso-fucking-lutely do! And you're right about the GPS on the chips. We have to disable them." I pause. "But that's more your expertise than mine."

Mike and Chase look at each other, and then Chase looks away, angling his neck to hide the scar. Mike reaches out and touches Chase's shoulder. "I'm still sorry about that. If I had known—" he doesn't finish.

"If either of us had known." Chase shakes his head. "Trust me, I know now. They spent a lot of time talking about what we'd done, and examining my neck and the rest of what's inside." He looks at us both. "It stays there, the rest of the network, like this tumor. Once they popped on a new chip, it started working again. So your point about them changing the game and up-grading the hardware is real."

"So what do we do?" I ask.

Chase looks around the room and then nods at the scalpel. "If we hit the right spot with that, we should be okay."

"You mean, we're going to put the scalpel into our neck and hope we hit the chip and not slip and kill ourselves."

"Pretty much."

I laugh, and Chase joins me, but Mike stares, wild-eyed. "I'm glad you two didn't know each other on the outside. You're both trouble. I can feel it."

"Trouble that's going to save your ass," Chase says. "Here, I'll go first, and show you it's not so bad. Kind of like going after a tick that's burrowed in."

"Have you ever done that, gone after a tick?" I ask.

"Hell, no. But you got the idea."

I do, but still think this is crazy, and yet know the clock is ticking. The crew is reviewing something on their tablets, while the good-hair guy is scrolling through his phone.

Chase grabs a scalpel and squeezes his neck. "Turn on the light."

I flip on the surgical lamp and Chase moves beneath it. Now that he's squeezed up his skin, the chip is visible. Opaque, but visible. "Just stick it into the center and hold it there for a minute."

"Like a reset button," I say.

"Sure." Chase hands the scalpel to Mike, who reaches up to his boyfriend's neck with a hand that shakes so badly I grab it from him without a word.

I spy the middle and jam the scalpel in. When I feel pressure at the tip, I hold it there for a moment and then pull it back out. Chase's neck blackens at the insertion point.

"Next," he yells and hops down.

"Are you okay?" Mike asks.

"*I'm* fine. But if this works, you two will be jonesing pretty hard, so we really do have to haul ass."

I need no more instructions, and let Chase get to work. He grabs the scalpel and kills the chip at my neck. I feel a mild sting and when I take my hand away from where he inserted the scalpel, my fingers are covered in black. Otherwise, there's no change.

It takes the both of us to kill Mike's chip. Chase holds his hands and looks him in his eyes while I do the work. A moment later, and we all stand, not dead, and hopefully, not traceable.

I check the monitor one last time before heading out into the hall. The crew is still there, so we have a chance. It's as desolate down here as when I first came, and in spite of my nerves, my stomach growls. "Soon, Kenny," Chase says.

"Do you have a place in mind?" I ask, and as I do, hope like hell that Chase isn't another pawn in this game, and that he's really only leading us to another layer of this entity.

"I do. It could get weird, but I've got a place." He looks up at Mike and then at me. "First, let's get the fuck out of here."

We find the stairwell and then tiptoe up. With each step the pressure in my chest builds. It feels as if when we reach the top, I'll either float away or explode.

Mike peers through the glass in the door. "The crew is packing up, but the door is still open. What's the plan?"

Chase looks at me and says nothing, so I throw out what I've got. "We bum-rush them and tear ass outside."

Chase shakes his head, and Mike follows his lead. "Subtlety, Kenny."

"Okay, so your plan?"

"We tell them we've been scheduled to be interviewed, and because they've been taking so long, they sent us to them."

"And then what?" I ask.

"Then we can simply walk out the door. We'll play the part of high-privilege patients, and no one will question a damn thing."

"That's how he ran shit, Kenny," Mike says. "Pure smoke and mirrors."

"Worked like a charm," Chase says.

"Until it didn't," I say.

"Well, if you have a better idea."

I don't, though. I just know that fifteen feet stand between me and the outside. And if we don't make it those fifteen feet, and then past whatever lies beyond, we're getting dragged back in and re-chipped and who knows what else. I like my chances better outside than in. "Lead the way."

Chase smiles, rubs the top of my head and then pushes through the door.

Every head at the end of the hall turns toward us. "There you are!" Chase says. "We've been looking for you."

We follow him toward the film crew and I spy the ward's cameras above us.

"You've been looking for us?" the good-hair guy says. He's still standing in the doorway, sunlight flooding around him.

"Yes. Hobson asked us to be interviewed, but then you guys went missing, so he sent us to find you."

If Chase never went to acting school, I'd be amazed. I know he's lying out his ass, but I believe him.

The crew looks at each other and then the guys shoulder their cameras. The good-hair guy shrugs and starts to step inside.

"The lighting is so much better out there," I say. "Don't you think we should use that as our background."

Chase shoots me a look and I can't tell if I've gone too far, or just added an awesome idea. Then the good-hair guy says, "Perfect," and leads us onto the platform at the top of the stairs. We huddle into the corner and one cameraman shoots us from a step below, while another from the doorway, where the good-hair guy stands. He picks up his mic.

"So, let's start with names. Who are you?"

This is fucking crazy. If we provide our names, there will be no doubt about who we are. Because if we pull this off, they're going to review this footage, and then they'll probably go to each of our homes, which, if Chase is thinking about his own, makes this a very dangerous play.

"I'm James Philmore," I say, using Big James's full name.

Mike stumbles, but manages to say, "And I'm Rashad Johnson."

Chase looks directly into the camera. "I'm Charles Ricci."

"All right, boys, so how are things here? You seem to be doing well."

I relax a bit while Chase launches into a complete bullshit story of his background and treatment here. I take the opportunity to spy the grounds. There's no fence, no barbed wire, just parking lot and a retaining wall that leads to Division Street. Beyond there is the city center.

"One question for all of you," the good-hair guy asks. "Did something happen, because you all have this smudge on your neck?"

In unison, we all reach up and touch our necks. Sure enough, my fingertips come back tinged in black. Chase is looking down, probably trying to figure out a lie, while Mike seems to hold his breath.

"We were carrying a piece of equipment on our shoulders. That's why we were in the basement," I say.

"But I thought you said you were looking for us? And what's in the basement?"

The questions hit like rapid fire and I look to Mike and Chase for support, but their eyes tell me to roll with it.

"Here, let us show you," I say, and motion for the camera guy beneath us to come up to the platform.

While he does, the good-hair guy says, "Are you sure you're allowed to bring us down there? We were told there was nothing worth seeing, which—to be honest—immediately set off my radar."

"Oh, there's stuff worth seeing, for sure. And we'll take you down, no worries. We're just doing what Hobson told us, so it's not like we're going to get in trouble."

"I like you, James." The good-hair guy claps my shoulder and then turns into the hallway, followed by the camera man who was beneath us.

"I like you, too," I say, before I slam the door closed.

Chase and Mike sprint down the stairs ahead of me, and when we reach the parking lot, Chase is out in front, scanning like a wild animal being hunted. Someone yells from behind us, but we know better than to look back. We jump the retaining wall at a dead sprint, having lost our slides on the way down the stairs.

The city sidewalk hurts beneath my feet, but there's no time for that concern right now. The three of us, dressed in all blue, do not blend in with the rest of the people who are out and about.

Sirens blast behind us and the people on the sidewalk are paying attention and looking around and pointing at the building. A couple sees us, looks toward the building, and then the husband slips out his phone. "Run!" I scream.

We do, and the pain is instant. I was never into sports and have always hated P.E., but Mike and Chase run as if they were on their schools' track teams. I keep up and we turn down a block and then over to another and the stitch in my side is splitting open. Sirens blare and tires squeal. I don't know where the hell Chase is leading us, because it's not as if safety is a point on a map.

Chase and Mike stop, so I stop. Chase puts his hands on his hips and looks around. "We're close," he says through heavy breathing. "I just don't know, exactly. It's been a while."

I'm sucking air so hard the only thing I can do is nod and force myself to stay upright. Passing out could occur at any second. More sirens join the wall of noise behind us, and I gather my breath and say, "Make a guess."

We take off again, and the city center bleeds into small houses and backyards, all broken down and uninhabited looking. Chase cuts down an alley and we follow him into a tiny backyard with a shed giving up its fight to a spider-like body of creeping vines. Chase steps through the vines and disappears. Mike parts the vines where Chase went, and I do the same.

It's like we're standing under a waterfall of green. Light slants in enough for me to see Chase opening a door on the side of the building. Mike and I follow him in. It looks like this used to be someone's man cave. There are couches and a TV and a bar in the corner. Everything is covered in dust. But the sirens have died away. The only sound is our heavy breathing.

"I used to crash here, sometimes." Chase sits on one of the couches. "If the GPS isn't working, we're safe."

"For now," I say.

Mike nods. "Was this the place you wanted to take us? Or do you have another in mind?"

"This is it."

"Good, because I don't think we can go home," I say. "They have to realize it was us. Or if they don't with that recording, they soon will."

Chase looks up at us. "Sit, would you?"

Mike and I both sit on another couch across from him. I look around, expecting someone to break in at any second. This is a good place to crash if they've lost us. But for how long?

"Let me level with the two of you," Chase says. "We're good for about twelve hours, and then the jonesing will kick in. Hard. So, we need to get our shit together, now, before that happens. If either of you has a place you think is safe, say so."

Mike stands and crosses to the other couch. "So long as I'm with you, it's going to be all right." He sits and they embrace and Chase strokes Mike's face.

"Except that it won't, honey. We need help. We're still addicts, and that piece of us that controlled the cravings and the voice for heroin is fried. We need a long-term solution."

Mike begins to cry and Chase tries to soothe him, but the point has settled and he's inconsolable. I lean my head back and try to see through to a way out, but if I could do that, I'd never have been here in the first place. As Mom would say, we've hopped from the frying pan to the flame.

I close my eyes and drift off to the sound of Mike's tears.

16

I snap awake and almost jump off the couch. Then I see Mike and Chase across from me, Mike sleeping on Chase's lap, and remember. I take in the room again, and it's darker, the minimal sunlight that was filtering in has faded. "How long was I out?"

"How many times have you had to ask that question?" Chase smirks. "About a half hour or so. This one is dead weight on me. It'll be fun waking him up."

I rub my face. "Sorry. I don't know what happened. Falling asleep while we're being chased is pretty damn stupid."

"Please. Your central nervous system just took a huge hit from disabling the chip, and then you followed it with an adrenaline rush. If you didn't pass out I'd be worried."

"Yeah, but you didn't."

"True, but I've been here before."

I know he doesn't mean the man cave, but I'm curious about where we are. "So this place is safe you think?"

"I've never had any trouble crashing here, and I spent a lot of nights on this couch. I think the home is foreclosed, and no one comes around, because who wants to buy a home, here?"

"You know the area, though. Were these the blocks you ran, or where you lived, too?"

Chase shifts Mike's head a bit so he can lean forward. "Full of questions, huh? I like that. No one's pulling one over on you."

I sit back. "You got me. But you know how it is. Can't trust anyone but myself, and when I'm using, I'm the last person I should be trusting."

"That's some solid advice. You read that somewhere?"

Chase's question reminds me of my uncle's journal, which is now property of the government.

"Who knows. After all the rehab facilities I've been to and therapists I've seen, that could have come from anywhere."

"You sound like me. Parents dumped all they had, and then some, into getting me better. None of it worked. How fucked up is that? All the money and compassion and care in the world, and there were only two things I cared about, H and this fool sleeping on my lap."

Chase strokes around Mike's ear and I'm momentarily jealous. I haven't had someone touch me like that—with true sensitivity—in forever.

"So, no, I'm not from here, but Northside. He's from here, which is why I probably ran so much in this neighborhood."

"Rich kid, then? Injury? Party? What got you hooked?"

"Rich as fuck. Dad's some financial guru to CEOs around the world. Parents are never home, so I threw all the parties. So, recreational. One night it was just there, and I had no one in my life to tell me not to, so I snorted. Within a month I was injecting. And then life fell apart. You?"

"Wisdom teeth." Chase laughs at this and then I tell him the rest of my story and he nods his head like he's heard it a dozen times, which he probably has, just like I've heard about the oh-poor-me-rich kids. But face-to-face, we're still the same—fucking junkies and lost causes. No wonder the government's trying to get rid of us.

"So, we've got less than twelve hours?"

"We do, and trust me, you don't want to feel what it's like to come down from this. The chip's been taking care of so much, physically and psychologically, that you aren't even aware of. After Mike fried it, I was a disaster, and scoring was the solution."

His words bring me back to Rashad's. "Rashad said you'd die if you used. But that's not the case?"

"I don't know who Rashad is, but clearly you don't die." He holds up his hands.

"He was on the ward."

"Huh?" Chase shrugs. "Maybe if someone injects you with a working chip, then yeah. But you won't want to use, so his logic is a bit off."

I think that so much of what we saw from Rashad was a lot off, because it wasn't him anymore. Who knows what was real and what wasn't. "What about now? Should we just use, even a little, to even out until we can figure out what we need to do?"

Chase smiles. "He was right, you and I would be class A felons together." Then he looks down at Mike. "No, and you've got to quit with that thinking. A little won't touch what you're about to feel, so it's pointless to consider.

You go all in one way or the other. There's no straddling the line this time around."

"And so if we don't find some kind of refuge, we're royally fucked?"

"Kenny, when they brought me back in they were terrible to me. Made me kick in that basement. No food. No water. No IV. The guards would come in and talk shit. They wanted me to die, I'm sure of it. If I could get my hands on *that* recording, I'm sure they'd shut the place down. Only thing that saved me was that they wanted to see if they could reboot my system. We go back after having escaped and killed the chip, I don't think you'll ever know who you are again. You'll either immediately be some cyborg, running his group of ten, or you'll be six feet under."

I hate that this is where we are and that I've also abandoned the guys like this. By now they probably have all been re-chipped and are back to learning the ward all over again, a place where most of them have been for months, with absolutely no contact with the outside world. How the fuck can this be legal? Isn't there a limit to an executive order?

"Chase, you got money and your family has connections, is there anyone that you can think of who would help us?"

"No. And I don't mean for that to sound harsh, but my family has written me off. If I don't come home sober, there's no point in coming home."

"And Mike, he's told me, he's been homeless for about a year. He's got no one?"

Chase kisses Mike's forehead. "I'm glad he confided in you. He must have seen something. But, yeah, he's got nothing. Which leaves us with you."

I nod, and then feel compelled to stand. It's as if I can hear the clock for our ten hours or so, clicking inside my head. I walk to the bar and idly trace swirls in the dust, trying to figure out who in the hell in my life might still be willing to help me. I think my parents might. It would take a lot of explaining, but their house is going to be under surveillance, I'm sure. So, wasted energy, there, because even if they agreed to help, what could they do?

My Uncle Theo could be an option if he didn't live so far away. There's no bus that can take us to him easily. I also wonder how he'd feel about my escape. Would he even believe me?

We need someone who will look after us, and it would be spectacular if that same someone could see if this chip is fully dead. I'm nervous that it's going to self-heal or some shit, or that we've only managed to turn off the GPS and not the other systems, which would mean no cravings, but would also mean the government still has the ability to fuck with our brains.

I need a compassionate tech geek.

And as if I've willed the memory to run, I see her. Michelle Haskins, seventh grade, Tech class, a goggle-wearing-computer-coding nerd of the best kind, who loved puppies and Pokémon.

"I think I might have someone."

"Fuck you. Just like that?"

I return to the couch. "Well, unless the government just planted the memory and will be waiting at her house."

Chase holds up a finger. "Fuck, there's that."

"But, if not, before I started using, there was this girl, and we had a connection, but it was like seventh-grade, you know? I don't even know if she still lives where she used to."

Chase stares at me until I have to look away. "Kenny, don't dismiss your feelings because they came from a sober kid in seventh grade. Those are probably more true than what I feel for Mike right now."

"You know I can hear you," Mike says, his voice muffled by Chase's legs.

"Oh, I do. Just wanted to see what you'd say. Go ahead, say it again. That felt good."

Mike laughs and Chase smirks his smirk, and I think about what he said, and how he's right. There's a chance. It's a longshot, but there's hope.

Mike sits up and Chase rubs his head and Mike swats his hands away. "Sorry for conking out like that," he says, looking at me. "But I did catch some of what you two were saying. And, yeah, we've got no one. Sorry, Kenny, but if there's even the slightest chance that this girl will help, we should go."

"What kind of neighborhood?" Chase asks.

"Suburban. Cul-de-sacs and all that."

"Perfect. If she can stick us in a shed or a basement and keep us alive until we're sober, we might just be okay."

"What about the rest of the shit still in us? Don't we need to worry about that?"

"Fuck, yeah. But one step at a time."

We are all quiet for a moment, contemplating this step, our next move, I'm sure, and then Mike says, "Let's raid the house, get whatever clothes and food we can, then maybe we can hotwire a car or some shit."

"One step at a time," Chase repeats, but this time pats Mike's hand.

* **

Raiding the house is shockingly easy. Chase was right, it seems as if whomever owned the place just walked away—or was forced to. The guy was older and much wider than any of us, but he was also pretty short. So, as much as Chase and I look like terrible thrift store shoppers, wanna-be hipsters, Mike looks like he may be homeless, again. The khaki pants he has on are high waters on him and so bunched at the waist, it's obscene.

We found some ridiculous T-shirts for beer companies, and old sneakers that also barely fit, but are better than nothing. The last touch are the hats. This guy has one hell of a collection, so we each found one, adjusted the snaps and have at least one article that fits right.

Chase raided the pantry and found a couple cans of raviolis that weren't expired, so we ate them straight out of the cans, cold, and they're the best thing I've eaten in forever. While I was raiding the old guy's sock drawer, I found a wad of bills. Only singles, and when all laid out only totaled $30. It's enough to get us bus rides to Michelle's, and some food. However, if we need to survive outdoors, because things don't work out with her, we'll need more.

"You ready?" I ask Chase and Mike, who both shake their heads, but then say, "Yeah."

We leave our blueberry outfits behind, buried in the bottom of the old man's drawer, and step out into the evening light. The sun's almost set and the sound of cars zipping down the road isn't far away.

We all brace for an assault when the door shuts behind us, but nothing happens—no cops, no SWAT team lying in wait for us, just the sound of crickets in the grass.

It takes three blocks for us to leave the dilapidated section of homes and re-enter the city center. Cop cars are parked along the intersections, but there aren't any roadblocks. "You think they're looking or are just showing a presence?" Mike asks.

"Hard to tell," I say, "but I don't think we should take the bus stop across the street." We hang in the shadowland that exists under a broken streetlight.

"Good call," Chase says. "We should probably split up, too. The three of us together looks obvious."

I look at the two of them and figure I'm the odd one out, but Mike moves first. "First bus stop past this one. Meet me." He lowers his head and pinches his shoulders up around his ears and takes off. He's a quarter of a mile away in minutes because of his insanely long stride. Chase and I watch him cross the street. The nearby cop car does nothing, and Mike recedes into the people out and about.

"Well, if the scarecrow can blend, so can we." Chase taps my side.

"Yeah, but he doesn't exactly blend in that outfit."

"He doesn't blend anywhere. It's what makes him special."

"You two, it really is a thing. He came into that facility with one goal in mind, to find you."

Chase looks away, but I can see the tears forming in his eyes. "He succeeded. And you're right, this shit is real, so we've got to follow this through, get clean, stay hidden. I'll do whatever it takes."

"Then you go first. I'll be right behind you."

He squares his shoulders to the street and then as if he's once again performing, swaggers away, saying, "Not if I see you first, fuckface."

I watch him go, and he passes the cops, and nothing happens. He touches his hat, like some old man as he goes, no doubt talking shit compliments to the women he's passing, because they turn and laugh and carry on. Mike was right about him. Smoke and mirrors.

I take a deep breath and walk slow. It's strange being outside, and beyond that, among people, again. Regular citizens, who are shopping or grabbing a bite to eat. Doing the things that the government would like from all of us on the ward. I think of Big James and Devon and Ramirez as I go. How in the hell is it fair for them not to have another chance at being themselves, at play-acting like Chase, or being this ultra-protective boyfriend, like Mike. And even Rashad. What's happened to him? Is he home now, all robotronically making his way through the evening with his family, a shell of his former self?

At the crosswalk I have to wait with the crowd, and a couple of people have their phones out. Two are looking at the same alert, something from the local news station. A video pops on and the reporter says, "Breaking tonight, three patients have escaped from the government's new heroin addiction facility, here in Washkill." The video cuts from the anchor to a field reporter who's stationed outside the facility, his face lit up by the camera lights.

"The patients escaped out of the facility through that door behind me, came down those stairs and crossed into the city center, where they disappeared." The video zooms in on the door and the stairs and then cuts back. "Director Tom Hobson could not be reached for comment, but a documentary team, who was filming at the facility, has shared video of what they say is an interview with the three escapees."

Before the video cuts to the footage of the interview, the light turns and the crowd moves with it. I can no longer see the video, but I can hear the audio. Our "interview" plays, followed by the reporter coming on to indicate that the names given are not our own. He then provides our real names and from what it sounds, also puts up a picture of each of us. "There's a ten-thousand-dollar reward for each patient, so call the number on the screen, contact the police at the email provided, or hit them up on social media."

I tuck my head away, like Mike did, and ignore the chatter of the two women who were watching. I need to find Chase and Mike and let them know. I pick up my pace as soon as I'm free of the crowd and turn over this plan. We could be caught before we even get out of town. We could get all the way to Michelle's and someone out walking their dog calls the cops and turns us in. Or, for the money, she could. Fuck! We might be better off just going home and saying one last goodbye to our families. But, no, that's only an option for me.

A couple miles up the road, I see the outline of a bus station. Mike and Chase are outside it, leaning against one another. Two people sit inside the shelter, both on their phones.

"Did you see the news?" I ask when I reach them.

"Yeah, just now." Chase indicates the people inside the shelter.

I move closer. "Did anyone give either of you a double-take?"

"No, everyone's glued to their phones," Mike says.

"For now, that's a good thing," I say. "You still want to go to Michelle's? The town could be crawling?"

"If we had another option, I might say no." Chase holds up Mike's hand. "But we don't. Wherever we are in the middle of the night, it's going to get real ugly. We may be in the woods, some shed, or even the comfort of Michelle's home, but at least we'll be together, and not in that facility."

I respect this. We have different motivations, but one unified goal—to stay out of the government's hands.

The bus rolls up, and fortunately, it's the right line, the one I've taken in and out of downtown so many times. We each peel out a couple bucks, get on, heads low, and make our way to the back. The lights dim when the bus accelerates away from the stop, but phones illuminate the faces of the passengers around us, and more than half are staring at our faces on their screens.

17

The bus stops at the one convenience store in town and we get off. I've scored here a few dozen times, have even shot up behind the building, sitting on pallets and nodding off against the wall.

"Home sweet home?" Chase asks after the bus has pulled away.

"Yeah. If we were to take the street over there and then make couple of rights and a left, we'd be at my doorstep."

"You weren't lying about this being the suburbs," Mike says. He's looking around, noticing that even though we're at a convenience store, with its bright lights, its dark everywhere else. There are no streetlights. All the cables are buried underground. We might as well be in the woods. "How far to this girl's house?"

"Closer than to mine," I say. "If she still lives there, it's over that way." I point toward her house, but it might as well be into a black curtain.

"Yeah, that helps." Mike claps me on the shoulder. "Show us the way."

We walk and are the only ones out, which I'm thrilled about, because escaping the city center without anyone seeing us was a miracle. Out here, though, people are a hell of a lot nosier, so we're dead in the water if seen. Which makes me wonder about my approach.

"Hey, how do you guys think I should, you know, start this conversation?"

Chase and Mike are just behind me, holding hands and swinging them. "You said you had a connection. What kind? How far did you go?" Chase asks.

"It was seventh grade. I think she was the girl I first noticed in that way. And so, we didn't really do anything. It was just a lot of awkwardness around each other because we'd been friends before, and then felt something else."

"But you were friends," Mike says. "That's good. You didn't like love her and leave her, you know?"

"No, I just moved onto a different scene, and she took the better path."

We're all quiet for a minute and then Mike says, "That's what you open with, then. She knows your past, probably knows you're in trouble, so you ask for help from a friend."

I turn around to see if he's fucking with me, because he sounds like every counselor, ever, but he and Chase have the same steadfast look.

When I turn back, we're at Michelle's street. "That's hers, the raised ranch in the middle."

In this light, as we approach, I can't tell if the Haskins still live here. Their name isn't on the mailbox, and it's not as if Michelle is a child and might have left her bike in the driveway. However, she is old enough to have just graduated, which sparks hope, because the sticker on the Subaru parked in the driveway reads: *My kid and my money go to RIT.*

I stare for a moment. RIT. Makes perfect sense that Michelle would make it into a school for technology, that she stayed smart and followed the course goals set forth for her by the same guidance counselor I ignored.

"You can do it, Kenny!" Chase whisper-yells from the end of the driveway, where they're hiding behind a bush.

I give them a thumbs-up and then head to the front door. As I climb the steps, though, running through what in the hell I'm going to say, I catch movement through the window to the left. Michelle's room was upstairs, along with her parents'. The downstairs had a guest bedroom in the back and a living room in the front, where I'm looking now. I come back down the steps and peer through the curtain into the room.

It's been transformed into some kind of workshop and my heart falls into my stomach. Whoever lives here now has abandoned the Haskin movie room and replaced it with whatever this is.

But then the movement comes back, and instead of running away, I stay and see what or who it is. The girl pulls her hair back, slips on goggles, and takes a seat at the stool. She's about to fire up whatever tool is in her hand—appears to be a soldering iron—but looks over her shoulder, instead. I'm frozen in place, because it's Michelle, but not the Michelle I remember. This woman is all business, her face pinched and goggles already fogged. I can't tell if she sees me or not, until she stands and comes to the window.

"And what in the fuck do you want?"

At this moment, to be anything other than who I am. "Michelle? It's Kenny. I need help."

She slowly takes the goggles off and then pulls out her phone. She shines the flashlight app in my face and then gasps. "No shit?"

"Yeah, so, hi. Sorry to creep up like this."

She moves the light away from my face, but keeps it on me. "You're a fugitive. What in the hell are you doing here?"

This is such a mistake. I feel the burn of it rise up in me and want to turn away, but I can't. There's nowhere to go. Then something clicks. I have something to offer that she might want.

"Michelle, I know it's been forever. Trust me, this is totally fucking weird, and I'm sorry for putting you in this position, but I honestly think you might like to see what's going on with me."

"Are you out of your fucking mind? Did you score already and are just wandering around town? I don't need to be any more informed about heroin than I already am, asshole."

I step back because of her vehemence, and because I don't understand this last part. "That's not what I meant, and no I'm not high. The government's filled me with this crazy ass technology, and," I wave toward her work station, "trust me, it's up your RIT alley."

Her eyes pinch. "How do you know I got into RIT?"

"The sticker." I shrug. "Seems like a good fit, though. I can't believe you don't have the movie room anymore."

"We haven't had that in years. After my cousin moved in—" She stops abruptly and turns away.

I know this Michelle. She's deliberating. I'm not sure if I should let her know I have friends, and that we're all going to get super sick in a few hours. I don't want to change her mind if she's willing to help.

"I could really use the money," she says, and must see my confusion, because she continues, "The reward money. Thirty-grand will pay for a lot of equipment."

"I...I...I'm only worth ten."

"You think I can't see the other two hiding behind the bush?"

We're even more fucked than I thought. "Listen. Help us. I meant what I said, you're going to want to check out this technology. But we're about to detox and we need somewhere safe. If you give us that, you can experiment all you want, and when you're done, fuck it, call the cops and claim your reward. But only for me. You don't know these guys, but I do, and they deserve a fresh start."

Michelle is quiet for a minute, mulling this over. She's always had that objective scientific mind, that, to be honest, I love, because it's exactly the opposite of my impulsive nature.

"You were like this back then. Selfless. Helpful. Cute. It's nice to see you haven't killed all of that with drugs."

"Thank you?"

"Don't thank me yet. It'll be a shock, but this isn't my first time helping someone get clean. Meet me at the shed out back." She moves away from the window and goes out her door.

I turn and wave to Chase and Mike. They walk up the driveway like they're scared of coming in after curfew. "She'll help us. We have to go to her shed in the back, which is where I'm guessing she'll have us get clean. But, she's also super smart and going to RIT, so she's going to want to look at whatever is in us."

"She can poke and prod and much as she wants," Chase says. "If she's willing to help, I'm her guinea pig."

"What he said. Show us the way," Mike says.

I nod and walk around the back of the house. Michelle's barely discernable next to the backyard shed, but as we get closer her wide eyes and intrigued expression are clear.

"Damn, Kenny didn't say anything about getting saved by some damsel," Chase says.

Michelle stares him down. "I may be a damsel, but I'm in no distress. That's you."

"Oh, she's sassy. This is perfect. I'm Chase, by the way. This is my man, Mike."

"Yeah, I know. I've seen your Wanted posters."

This brings us all up short. Because that statement combined with us getting into a wooden box, feels a hell of a lot like she's a bounty hunter.

"Are you really going to help us?" Mike asks, and it has that pure innocence-tinge that is nearly impossible to bear.

"I am," Michelle says. "But there's one of me and three of you, and no offense, you're not exactly trustworthy. Not yet. You help me, help you get clean, then you have nothing to worry about."

I trust her, but even if I didn't, what other options do we have? So, I step inside the shed first to demonstrate that I'm committed. Chase and Mike take a moment, but follow me.

"And if we don't help?" Chase asks.

"Then you're money in the bank." Michelle closes the door and the sound of a padlock clicking shut, follows. "Night boys. I'll check on you in the morning."

We stand still, trapped again. Then Chase says, "Well, this will be cozy."

Amid the lawnmower and snow blower and stack of wood and various tools, there's barely enough room for one person to sit, let alone the three of us, especially with Mike's size, but we manage.

"She seems nice," Mike says.

"Yeah, I get the whole nerdy girl thing. She's badass, Kenny. You had taste," Chase says.

I shift to my side to get comfortable. "My whole fucking life is in my past. You know? Had. I had a lot. Look at me now."

"Preaching to the choir," Chase says.

"I ain't ever had shit," Mike says, "and yet I know how much I still lost."

It's a powerful truth that we all sit with for a while. Then I say, "Thanks for trusting me. Thanks for not up and running or ditching me in the city. You two could make it together, I know it."

"We owe *you*," Mike says. "We're all in this shit. That's the one thing I think the program had right. You know, the one in ten piece. I can respect that. Sure, you're gonna have assholes pull you down, but you can also have guys like you who will push you up."

"Exactly," Chase says. "Mike and I would fuck it up. For sure. It's what we do best. We need you, Kenny. It's going to be a long night, so hold onto that."

I have nothing left to offer, because I'm exhausted, and because I can only hope they're right. The one thing I have been consistently good at is letting people down. These truths that they don't tell you, like *drugs are fun*, also apply to yourself, like *you may actually be an asshole*. Seems like I've got this one last chance to find out who I am without drugs and without technology. Just me, running me own life. That's the goal.

18

Chase wasn't lying. I am a puddle of sweat, filled with tremors, completely unable to do anything but lie on my side and hold my stomach. I thought I'd already done this, the lying on the bed and pissing out my ass, but that was the government letting me believe I was detoxing, letting the chip get to work. This many days later, I can't have much left in my system, but Chase's voice is soothing as he checks on us and lets me know that I'm right, I should be okay, soon. Mike, however, is crying and moaning.

Consciousness comes and goes, as night deepens. Mike's shaking so bad, the tools on the wall next to him are knocking together. I worry that Michelle's parents are going to hear and come check on the shed, but nothing happens. Chase moves the tools and the noise goes away. Mike cries out, but Chase attends to him, having him bite down on his shirt that he's taken off.

My stomach cramps in waves, and I'd kill for the anti-nausea pills they give you. They're like magic. But even better would be some H. I know Chase told me to stop thinking like that, but it would help. I would no longer be in pain. But that's the short game. I've got to start learning to play the long game.

Light appears through the chinks in the shed's siding. I don't understand what's happening at first, but as it brightens, I say to Mike, "Hey, man, it's morning." My voice is sandpaper, but I know the worst of the physical pain is over.

"We gonna make it, Kenny," he says, and it sounds as if it takes all of his energy to utter those words.

I look over and see that Chase is slumped against the wall, sleeping. He must be worn out as well. But he's done this, on his own, in the basement. He's strong enough to help us see the rest of this through.

The sound of the padlock being jostled and then popped open scares me, but then Michelle is standing outside in the morning light, holding a plate of toast and a pitcher of lemonade. "Looks like you all survived."

I pull myself to a seated position and it's a real struggle. Chase lifts Mike up and he leans against the wall.

"Brought you something to help with your energy. I know you probably aren't hungry, but others who have kicked tell me that they can stomach toast and lemonade." She sets the plate on the seat of the ride on mower and then the pitcher and cups on the hood.

"Others?" I ask.

Michelle squats down to look me in the eye. "It's not like people want their kids going where you went. People are taking matters into their own hands."

"Even though it's illegal?" Chase asks. He grabs a couple slices of toast and gives one to Mike and one to me.

"Risk to value, that's it," Michelle says. "There are rumors about what's going on inside those places. People are scared." She looks at me. "Which is why I'm intrigued about the tech inside you, because that's one of the rumors that scares me most."

"It's no rumor," Chase says. "You can see for yourself. Just need a strong light."

Michelle's eyes stay steady on him, while she seems to think this over. Then she stands. "Finish your breakfast, and we'll see how you're feeling around lunch time. One of the strongest lights I know will be shining above, then." She steps out and locks us back in.

I take a bite of my toast, and it goes down all right, so I take another. She's buttered it just the way I like it, and before I know it, I've devoured the entire slice. I skootch up and fill a cup with lemonade. It's tart and super sweet, but feels wonderful on my hoarse throat.

"Good call coming here," Mike says, his voice a little stronger.

I turn and he's eating as well. We air-cheers with our cups. "How much longer until we're strong again?"

Chase swallows. "Probably a few days. We have to take it slow, which considering we're locked up shouldn't be a problem. I think we'll be fed, but we're going to have to figure out how not to think about drugs."

"Literally the hardest part of all this," I say.

"Yup," Mike agrees. "Maybe we can mow the lawn, do some landscaping."

We all laugh and I say, "And then we can swing by for a visit at my parents.'"

"Shit, we are cutting it close for you, but think about how happy they'll be once they see you clean," Chase says.

"True, but I wonder how that works. We're fugitives now. For how long? Forever?"

"One day at a time," Mike says, and we eat our toast and drink our lemonade and try to find something else to occupy our brains, aside from dead technology and the nagging of our former lover.

By noon, we're starting to lose our minds, and the shed smells like our sweaty asses and the piss that splashed back when we tried to get it out one of the holes. Michelle opens the door and then reels back. "Shit, I need to hose you off. When's the last time you showered?"

None of us answer, because we don't know.

"Ugh, it's worse than I thought." She heads back into the house and returns a couple minutes later with towels, soap, and shampoo. She sees us still sitting inside and says, "You can come out. It's safe."

"Is it?" I ask.

"Yeah, so long as you stay in the backyard. My parents are at work."

Michelle's house sits on a few acres of land, the back of which buts up to the woods. It used to be fun coming here, because the trails are amazing. We'd spend all day looping through them, lost but happy.

Chase helps both Mike and I stand and then walk out into the bright light. The sun is a bit more than I can handle, so I stare at the ground and watch my feet trample the lawn.

"Strip down and I'll get you rinsed," Michelle turns on the hose and tests the spray nozzle.

I look at Mike and Chase. They hesitate as well. Michelle scowls.

"If you want help, you have to get clean. I don't care if you leave your underwear on."

I sigh and step out of the old man's pants and pull off the shirt. Then I look down at the shitty, government-issued drawers I have on and say fuck it. Let her see me naked. I've been way more embarrassed in my life.

"Damn, Kenny, you're almost as pasty as me," Chase says.

"Funny. Did you take your underwear off, or are you that white?"

Mike laughs but Chase whips off his underwear and throws them at my head.

A quick spray of cold water keeps me from throwing my own. "Easy, boys." Michelle tries to scowl while she says this, but her mouth is pulling up at the edges. Then she aims the nozzle at us.

She hits us with the hose before we have a chance to brace for the water and it stings. But I bend and let her get my hair as well, and in a minute, I'm soaking wet and cold. She throws the soap to Mike, who starts lathering. He passes it to Chase when he's done and then he gives it to me and I lather as quickly as possible. I want this over ASAP.

We repeat the process with the shampoo and then Michelle blasts us again with the water, and her lawn is soon covered with white foam. She brings us the towels once we're good and clean, and they are like the toast from this morning, perfect. We stand in the sun for its warmth and dry off. I don't want to put on the old man's clothes, again, but since we have nothing else, I slide back in, but go commando.

We sit at the patio set and Michelle brings out peanut butter and jelly sandwiches and apples. "Eat, and tell me what I'm supposed to find," she says.

I hate that we've shown up like this and she's waiting on us like this is her job, but this isn't her first time at the rodeo, I guess.

"Well, just beneath here," I say, pointing to the mark left from when we disabled the GPS, "you'll find a chip that's connected to this implant, of sorts. The chip runs the system, while the implant grows and becomes a part of your nervous system. It can override things, like wanting to do drugs."

Michelle nods, but her face is straight poker. "So, why is this bad?"

"Because it's capable of more than just overriding addiction issues. It changes you completely." I look over at Chase. "He went through the program, got out, and didn't even remember Mike."

"He was like a zombie or some shit," Mike says. "I had heard about the chipping, the rumors, like you, so I took a chance and put a magnet up to his neck." He turns to me. "Sorry I lied about that earlier, Kenny. Didn't know if I could trust you."

"No worries. Finish your story."

Mike turns back to Michelle. "So I put the magnet up to his neck, and the shit blew up. He became himself again. He came back to me."

"But you ended up back inside?" Michelle asks.

"Government came and got me. Can't have a broken cyborg out there. Who knows what could happen?" Chase says.

Michelle looks at Mike and me. "And you two?"

"Roommates. We started to notice the weird shit that was going down, and he was already on the hunt for Chase, so we tested the waters too much, and they were about to upgrade our chips when—"

"When the film crew came through and you broke out." Michelle cuts me off.

"You saw that?"

"Impossible not to. That alert is everywhere."

"So why aren't the cops here? You sitting across from thirty-grand," Chase says.

Michelle looks down at the table for a moment, and when she looks up there's a ferocity to her that I remember, but haven't seen in forever. It's breathtaking. "My cousin, Andrew, went in about six months ago. We tried to help him, here. He moved into the downstairs, my workshop now. He couldn't get clean, just kept escaping and going on benders. One day he destroyed the downstairs, because we'd locked the door, like I do with the shed, now. Busted everything, walls, windows, door. After that, my parents let him get picked up, while I turned the room into my workshop." She pauses. "Andrew was the sweetest kid I've ever known. That wasn't him who destroyed the room. That was his addict. And he's worth a shit ton more than ten-grand. So, if it were him sitting across from me at this table, I'd say Andrew, let me have a look at your neck. Don't worry about me selling you out."

I stand up and move into the sun. Despite her earlier statement, Michelle brings a flashlight with her, and puts it behind my neck, just beneath my ear. "Tell me if I hurt you," she says and then proceeds to move the light and twist my neck. Her forehead is creased and she bites her lip. She grasps the implant with her fingers and massages it. Even though this hurts a little, I don't say a word. I enjoy the sensation of having someone's hands on me that aren't hell bent on causing me pain.

A few minutes later she rests her arm at her sides and switches off the flashlight.

"What do you think?" I ask.

"You said they were going to upgrade you, but you avoided that how?"

I turn away. "I injected the doctor with the anesthesia she was going to put in me."

"Really? How?"

"I stuck it in her jugular when she wasn't looking."

"Shit, Kenny."

I turn back. "I know, but desperate times and all that. I promise, I'm not going to do anything like that to you. Poke and prod and examine all you want. You can have Mike and Chase hold me down."

"I believe you. It might be a stupid thing to believe, but I do. You remember Andrew?"

"No, we never met."

She sighs. "He would have done something like that. Self-preservation is a strong thing to kill, Kenny. There's hope for you."

Michelle taps my chest and her hand at my heart makes it flutter.

"Let's go to the shop," she says to all of us. "I want to try something."

We follow her inside, and the room I saw from the window last night is much more intricate than I realized. Michelle has a couple of computers, so many different kinds of cables, and enough random parts to build a robot, it seems.

"What engineering program are you entering?" Chase asks, while he looks around the room, at all of the parts, and barely anywhere to sit.

"Mechanical," Michelle says. "I mean, I have a love for electrical and computer, but so much of that you can teach yourself. I don't have access to the big machines, and really, that's the next wave. A.I. is around the corner."

"I think it's already here" Mike says.

"Let's find out. Kenny, sit." She clears off a space on a stool next to one of her computers. "If you didn't do too much damage, I might be able to connect to the system and get a sense of what's occurring."

"Does that mean you're going to cut open my neck?"

"You said you'd let these two hold you down." Michelle smirks.

"Did he?" Chase leans over me. "You dirty boy."

"I meant for this." I look over at Chase. "So, if you and Mike will do the honors."

Mike and Chase each grab a shoulder, and I'm pleased with how much better we all smell. This would have been disgusting an hour ago.

The aroma of alcohol is strong, and when I look up, Michelle is wiping down a scalpel. "Where'd you get that?"

"Really? All of this tech in this room, and you want to know where I bought this?" Michelle laughs. "Marlon's Pharmacy, in town."

She puts the scalpel down and gathers up a cable and connector. Then Michelle logs onto her computer and plugs the cable into the USB. She finds some program and then turns back to me. "This is really simple, Kenny, and shouldn't take long at all. I am going to cut you open and then attach this to the chip in your neck." She holds up the other end of the cable and it's incredibly unremarkable, considering what I imagine it's going to do. "The program will then scour for whatever it can and download it, here. Once that's done, I'll pop this off you and put some Crazy Glue over the incision. You'll be good as new."

I doubt this. Not the tech part, but the good as new part. Michelle seems to have an incredible belief in herself and others. I wish I shared that. Maybe in a few days, when the idea of heroin stops slipping in. Well, I guess, *if* that ever happens.

"Ready?" Michelle puts on gloves and looks at Mike and Chase and in response they apply more pressure to my shoulders.

She looks at me and asks the same question. I nod and so does she, and then I feel the white-hot pain of her cutting through to whatever lies below. She dabs around my neck, no doubt at the blood that's dribbling, but then I can feel her insert the cable into my neck. It brings a new wave of nausea, but I grit my teeth and bear it. "You're doing great, Kenny," she says.

I keep my eyes closed and try to find a happy place. Everything I have that's good is from childhood, and since I'm at Michelle's, it's no surprise that I go to a time when we used to hang out, a time when she looked at me and thought I was cute.

One day, after school, seventh grade. We were walking home and our hands bumped each other. Our pinkies set off fireworks between us, and even though we both laughed, a minute later, we were holding hands. Those same hands that are now trying to decipher what's in me, and that same voice is now saying, "Holy fucking shit!"

I look up at her monitor and the ward comes back into view. There are a thousand tiles on her frame that seem to cover my entry to just before my departure.

"Is that video?" Mike asks.

Michelle clicks on the first tile and, indeed, a video of me, in the detox room plays:

"Sedation?" the nurse says.

The image of me nods.

"No. That's not how we do things here at Ward 15. Welcome to the new protocol of addiction recovery."

The nurse's hand reaches down and cups my knee.

"I know you're probably used to a lot different treatment, but that treatment clearly hasn't worked in the past or you wouldn't be here. Don't look so surprised."

Michelle looks at us. "Is this the program?"

I can feel Mike and Chase nodding above me. "What does that mean?" I ask.

Michelle seems to pull herself away from the screen and looks at me, her face squirming with questions. "We have a record of your entire time on the ward. Video. Audio. For whatever reason, the system needs all of this."

"Why? What's the point?" Chase asks.

"It must need the data over a period of time." Michelle clicks around the screen. "You were there a while, Chase, why do they need you there for so long, if the chip controls your cravings?"

"It's their model. One in Ten. We're responsible for one another, and if one messes up, it screws everybody in the ten up. Even after they're released."

Michelle taps her front tooth with her finger. "That's a hell of a system to keep you there, isn't it? And it provides the thing still left in you time to grow."

"What else?" I can see in her face that there's more she's thinking, and not saying.

"I could be wrong, but this data could be used to form a sort of memory. If so, I bet the government can access this and cherry pick what you do and do not remember."

"Could they still access us, now?" Mike's question strikes at my fear.

"I think so," Michelle says.

"Then what do we do now?" The cable bobs along with my question.

"I can try to shut it down. We could take it out. Or we could do nothing, see what happens."

As much as I like the third option, that method hasn't really worked well in my life, so it will have to be whichever Michelle thinks she is capable of.

Just as I'm about to ask, the sound of a car pulling into the driveway fills the room, followed by the pop of a door.

19

The front door opens and Michelle's mom calls out, "Honey, are you here?"

Michelle stands, crosses to the door and then comes back. "Shit, I can't have her come down here. I'm going outside. Do *not* open this door." She pulls the workshop door closed behind her. Chase, Mike, and I listen to the footsteps above. They move back down the stairs, and Michelle's mom calls for her.

We are completely fucked if her mom comes through that door. I have one hand on the cable, ready to tear it out and run if I have to, when Michelle's voice calls from the back. "Mom? That you?"

From just outside the workshop door, Michelle's mom's muffled laughter is audible. Then she calls out. "I thought you were in the workshop, since that's where you spend all your time."

Michelle answers from closer to the house now. "I was getting some sun. What are you doing home?"

"Good, you need some vitamin D."

I'm staring at the door, trying to envision the conversation occurring beyond it. Michelle's mom is a sweetheart, and was always full of exited energy. Hearing this exchange makes me wish for a lot of things, and seeing my parents is right up top. But so is being someone they want to see, which I am not yet. In spite of what we're figuring out here, my urges for H have not gone away. And in spite of what we do, I'm sure they're only going to get worse.

"I forgot my lunch," Michelle's mom says. "But, now that I'm here, I kind of think I did it on purpose, so I could come home and check on you."

"I'm fine, Mom."

"Well, you are outside, so that's a good start, but it could be dangerous out there."

"What? During the day? We're near the woods, not in the middle of nowhere."

One of them leans against the wall. Chase, Mike, and I all sit up at the noise.

"I'm not worried about a bear or anything," Michelle's mom says. "But that Kenny boy is on the loose. You saw the news."

"I did. And why would he escape that place and then come home? I'm sure he realizes it's not safe here."

"You don't know that, so please just be aware of your surroundings. Especially if you're outside. Which, again, you should be doing. That workshop's like an addiction for you."

"Whatever. Enjoy your lunch." Michelle's voice carries down the hall, followed by the sound of the back door opening and closing.

"I didn't mean anything by it," her mom calls to her.

But she did. Chase, Mike, and I look at each other and we know. That kind of comment, that little dig, those are the points that stick in you forever. I'm in no position to feel sorry for anyone, but I do feel a moment of sorrow for Michelle. If it's true that this room has become her entire life, then it's kind of sad. But not in the way the three of us are sad. At least her addiction has a purpose behind it and could be used for good.

A few minutes later, Michelle's mom's car pulls out of the driveway and Michelle comes back into the workshop, her shoulders slumped.

"You okay?" I ask.

She looks at her computer. "Just Mom being mom. You know."

"We don't, actually," Mike says. "So, if you want to vent, go for it."

Michelle keeps her eyes trained on the computer and the quaver in her voice is barely perceptible, but it's there. "She just doesn't understand that this is what I'm good at. I'm not one of those kids who gave a shit about prom and the jocks and even getting good grades. I did well so that I can pursue this without breaking the bank. I'm kind of doing her a favor, but she doesn't seem to appreciate it."

"Well, I appreciate your skills," I say. "I mean, I'm hooked on this." I hold up the cable to emphasize the joke and see Michelle turn. She sees it and gets it and allows herself the laugh, and for those tears to fall.

"I'm not crying over her. It's your stupid joke." Michelle wipes her eyes.

"He does have a terrible sense of humor," Mike says. "Try living with him."

"Do you want me to create a highlight reel of his worst ones?" Michelle asks, pointing at the screen.

We all laugh at this, but then the seriousness of the moment returns. "So, what do you think is the best choice?" I ask.

"Removing it, but I don't think I can. I'm not a surgeon. The best I can do is wipe whatever's there, basically clean out the system, and we can hope that means you are no longer connected."

"But you can't be sure?"

"We'll find out one way or another, right?"

Even though it's a shitty situation, she's regained some of her composure and I'm glad for that and whatever help she can provide. "All right, then, do your magic."

Michelle taps at her keyboard and I stare at the ceiling and hope that this buys me enough time to finally get clean, and then maybe, just maybe, I can find a happy ending to this nightmare of my life.

***

It doesn't take Michelle long to do her thing, and soon, I'm disconnected, and Chase is patching me up with Crazy Glue, while Michelle disinfects the end of the cable with rubbing alcohol. Mike barely flinches when she cuts into him and then repeats the process of downloading and wiping the system. By the time Chase is finished, it's late afternoon and we are all exhausted.

We stare at the monitor, which now has the history of our time with the program. It's powerful information, but not anything that I would even know what to do with. And with how worn out we are right now, there's no energy for the conversation.

"Unfortunately," Michelle says, "there's a good chance that my dad will want to mow the lawn when he gets home, so you're going to have to hang out in the woods until the coast is clear."

Mike and Chase nod and I ask for Gatorade or water, whatever she has. Michelle sets us up with Gatorade and snacks and then asks me if I remember the trails at all.

"Vaguely," I say. "Why?"

"I haven't been back there in forever. My mom is kind of right about things, but, regardless, the tree house might still be there."

There's a twinkle in her eye when she says this, and I understand why. We didn't build the tree house or anything. It was there when we started playing in the woods, but it did become our kind of sanctuary. We'd play and then gravitate toward the treehouse without even having to speak about it. On hot days, or rainy days, or into evenings when we didn't want to go home. I've forgotten so much of who I used to be because of all of my drug use. Coming to Michelle's has been like swiping through a photo album.

"Well, I'll let you know, later. That is unless you want us to stay out there."

"No, no. Come back. You'll get eaten alive by mosquitos. And you three still need to be locked in. I'm not an idiot, I know you still want to use. You've got a long way to go."

"I do. We do. So, thanks, especially if I forget to say that again. You're pretty amazing, Michelle."

She turns away. "Go, before you're spotted by the suburbanites drinking their afternoon beers out on their patios."

I lead the way and the trails are as I remember them, but smaller. As we head up one slope, a new development is visible. One that's at least new since I was back here last. I turn one way, and then the next, and spy the oak tree with the gnarly limb. It's this giant, bulbous thing, that was a trail marker for us. Another twenty steps down the trail and we come to the tree house. It's a bit dilapidated, missing some of the roof and a section of siding. But the ladder up to it is still intact, and the floor is large enough to hold the three of us.

We each claim a section, open our drinks and snacks, while the din of lawnmowers rises in the distance.

The snacks are perfect and the coolness of the shade of the treehouse is just right, so that in no time I'm kind of blissed out, just staring into the patch of woods I can see. I should be scared. From the sounds of it, the police, the government—someone—is looking for us. I don't know what we're going to do when we're found. It's not a matter of if. Michelle's been phenomenal. This is the best turn of luck I've had in years, but we can't expect her to do any more than she's done, and at some point, we have to figure our way out of this mess.

And, yet, beneath it all, my mind's mapping out where my dealers might still be, or who I might be able to connect with. These trails don't terminate in here, but lead to other sections of town. This could be good.

"What you thinking about?" Chase asks.

I look over and he's talking to me.

"Spaced out a bit, sorry."

"Yeah, but I know that look." He elbows Mike. "You know that look."

"Sure do. How many spots you come up with?" Mike asks.

"What are you talking about?" I say, but do not look at either of them.

"Fuck, you, Kenny, yes you do. Where you gonna score?"

I whip around. "Why, you want in?"

Both Mike and Chase freeze for a moment, a decision is being made. "Yes," Mike says, "but we aren't going there."

"*We* as in the two of you?"

Mike looks down at the floorboards and shakes his head. "No, Kenny. None of us are. You've made it this far. We all have. There's no way we're letting you throw this all away."

"What about you, Chase? Don't you want to see what I can get?"

"Hell yeah, I do, and if you keep bringing it up, we might have no choice but to find out." He leans closer to me. "But here's the thing. *I* don't want to find out, if that means losing this."

"We're in a fucking tree, about to go back to a shed. What's there to lose?"

"I swear to God, Kenny, you keep talking like this—" Mike's voice is a growl.

"What? What will you do? Kick my ass?" I hate how my own voice sounds as these words fly out. They're not me. I'm barely me.

"No. I'll let you do that for yourself. Let you go find the dealer you're thinking about, who may or may not still be around. We'll let you walk out into the town that hates you, where everyone's watching their TV just wishing you'd come walking across the lawn. Like a reward they deserve for putting up with all your shit in the past. They'd call the cops in a heartbeat, probably pin you to the driveway while they wait. And all for what? To get high? Haven't you been high enough times? Can't this escape, this second chance, be enough for you? Shit, you walked straight into a girl who's helped you like this, and one who still seems to dig your sorry ass." Mike pauses, looks up and then delivers his conclusion. "Fuck you, Kenny, if you think you don't deserve better. Or that you don't owe some gratitude."

Mike sits back and buries his face in the crook of his arm. Chase rubs his back.

"On a scale of one to ten, how much do you want to use?" I ask.

"Like a motherfucking eight!" Mike screams. Birds fly up from their nearby perch. A lawnmower stops its whine. Something crashes in the woods, and Mike's echo dies out.

I'm so upset my hands are shaking. I might have a panic attack with the way my heart's racing. Chase grabs our hands. "Breathe, you two. Just breathe. We're safe. You don't need to score. Just feel this emotion, and know it will pass."

He sounds like a fucking counselor, and he's definitely acting like one. He's got his eyes closed, modeling our behavior. But I follow along, because there's nothing else to do. I know he's right. I know every person who's ever told me to knock it the fuck off has been right. Easier said than done.

I breathe and I think about my parents. I breathe and I remember Michelle. I breathe and a flash of a party comes to mind, and I remember myself in the mirror, the charcoal drawing from the program. I can still remember. The good and the bad. It's not all gone, wiped out by some chip. I'm still here. Unfortunately, with my addict.

I open my eyes, and the sun has drifted below the horizon. The sky has an orchid hue. Mike and Chase are still breathing deep, still trying to get calm. I have this sensation of drifting away from them. It's momentary, but peaceful. It feels right. The two of them going together. So long as it isn't back to the program, it'll be all right.

"Thanks, Chase," I say.

"You're welcome. Now stay calm, think about where you want to go after this."

I appreciate the invitation to distraction, but right now I'm not capable of thinking about my future. I can only handle the here and the now, and so I comb my mind for anything that will ground me.

An image appears. My uncle's journal. The one I left on the ward during our escape. The one I'll probably never see again. But I've got the one page I did read committed to memory, and I tease over my uncle's tenants:

1. Honesty, at all times, with yourself and others.
2. A mind works best when it's open, so drop your judgment and your preconceptions.
3. You are your surroundings, so be sure that who and what are

around you reflect what you want to see in yourself.

4. Avoid temptations of all varieties, because if there is no spark, you cannot have fire.

5. Believe in something greater than yourself. This doesn't have to be God, but it does have to possess the same power as one.

Based on his principles, I'm doing all right. I have all but the last one covered, but if I really think about it, Michelle kind of fits. She's not a god or anything, but she does have power and I do believe that I was pulled here for some reason. Call it divinity or dumb luck. Either way, I'm not slowly succumbing to the chip, the program, the government's plan. That's something to be proud of, and I am, but the addict in me wants more. I'll just have to divert his attention to something positive. If I can.

A while later and the lawnmowers are no longer singing their song. Echoes of families outside bounce back and forth among us. The aroma of dinners being cooked on grills waft over and my belly grumbles. I hope Michelle has food to spare.

A little while after that, the mosquitos attack from all directions. We tuck into our clothing to avoid the onslaught.

When there are no more voices from the backyards, we climb out of the treehouse. Wordlessly, and as quietly as possible, we make our way back to the shed. I grip the corner and peer into the yard. It's dark, and there's no one around, so I dart to the door and slip in. Mike and Chase follow me, and we sit, and we wait, and nothing happens.

I'm itching all over. Every part of me wants to run screaming from the shed. Because I need to score or get food or get away. I don't know. My brain is scrambled and I can't calm down. Mike or Chase grips my shoulder. I don't turn to see who, but after a while I do pat the hand to let them know I'm all right. To say thank you.

The door opens and Michelle appears with a plate of food, more lemonade, and a flashlight. She sets the flashlight in the corner, like a lantern, and then puts the food on the mower's seat, again.

We don't need directions, or to be told to go easy. We're starving and tear into the cold hamburgers and potato chips she's brought.

"Did you make these?" Chase asks around a mouthful of food.

"My mom. But I did grill them."

"Well, my compliments to the chefs, then."

"Won't your mom ask about the leftovers?" I ask.

"She might, but Dad loves his midnight snacks. I can always blame him."

We finish our food and drink the lemonade and feel infinitely better. But there's a pensiveness to Michelle. Like she's on her tiptoes.

"What is it?" I ask.

"You want the good or the bad?"

"Shit." I turn to Chase and Mike.

"The bad," Mike says. "Leave us with something good."

"Okay." Michelle nods, seems to gather her words, and then says, "They've upped the bounty on all of you. It's up to twenty-thousand, each."

Chase whistles. "Damn. If I could get the reward, I'd turn myself in."

"It's crazy. My parents can't stop talking about it because of Kenny."

"Are they hoping that I'm on my way home?"

Michelle looks me straight in the face. "Everyone in town is. There's a cop car parked outside your parents, and they're patrolling non-stop."

I look at the floor. It's oil stained and slightly damp, a couple years away from needing to be replaced. Twenty thousand would replace a lot of sheds. Would help with college. Would pay off some debts.

"We can't stay," I say. "It's too much of a risk."

Michelle grabs my arm. "Wait. That was the bad news. There's still good."

I open my mouth to speak, but Chase says, "Let her finish."

I back off and Michelle continues. "It's not good, like, woo! But I think it could be helpful." Her eyes dart over the three of us. "I reviewed all the footage. From each of you."

I can't imagine what she's thinking, seeing the place where the government believes we belong, vicariously mixing with people she's spent her life avoiding.

"Here's the thing. The government has commercials now, and their website is full of the same propaganda. They're selling it like it's this perfect answer, and that you will all come out clean and be these amazing members of society. It's like you go in a mess, and then come out like something from *Westworld*."

Mike, Chase, and I nod at this. That is pretty much the goal. Except for when the machines become sentient.

"But that's not at all what I saw. It was a total mind-fuck in there. And the GPS tracking, and the way they can know if you've used, that has to be against the law."

"Executive order and all that," I say. "We sign off, apparently."

"Yeah, about that. I highly doubt that would hold up in court if challenged. Think about it. What strung out kid, who's eighteen, knows what he's signing? What parent even understands? The duress around both is unreal. There's an executive order in place. The government has control. Therefore, you have no options even before you sign. How is that fair?"

"Damn, Michelle, if engineering doesn't work out, think about being a lawyer," Chase says.

Michelle's smile shines in the dim light.

"How is this good, though?" I hate to ruin her happiness, but I'm having trouble understanding the benefit.

"I'm not a lawyer, but it seems to me that if the footage was put in the hands of someone who is—I don't know—some group that cares about human rights, like the ACLU, and the three of you could corroborate it, this could provide what they need to open an investigation."

"But why? What good would that do?"

Michelle looks at me sideways. "Do you really think the shit they're doing is okay?"

"Not that it's okay, but are people really going to get up in arms about it? The entire reason this all came to be is because we, as addicts, suck. We're a 'drain on society.' I understand that you think it's terrible, and the three of us agree, but getting things to turn around just because the government isn't being transparent about their actions? Yeah, I can't see that happening."

We're quiet for a moment and then Michelle looks directly at me. "Do you really think this little about your self-worth?"

"He really does," Chase answers. "I haven't known him long, but Kenny clearly hates himself."

It hurts to hear, but I have no defense. He's right.

Michelle slips a finger under my chin, pulling my eyes up to hers. "Kenny, you are still the same boy who kissed me back in the day. You are still the same person who loves puppies and hates thunder. Just because you've spent the past few years trying to destroy that person doesn't mean you've succeeded."

I don't want to cry. I can feel them forming, but I'm trying to pull away, jumping, like a fish on a hook.

"Give me a chance to figure this out. Another day. It might only take one email. You owe me that."

I don't know how Michelle knows I want to run, to flee this scene of emotions and honesty, but I do. I want to sprint as fast as I can. But then I remember what she said about her cousin, and I remember everything she said about me. It's all true. That boy in me is about to turn into a puddle. That boy in me is agreeing with Chase and with Mike and with Michelle. I just haven't realized he's still here, buried under all the pills and alcohol and heroin. I do owe people, him especially. And I am grateful for this help, this chance to meet myself again.

"Okay," I say, because I can't get anything else out. I fall into Michelle, and that hook pulls clear, and my tears lurch out and onto her shoulder, while she holds me.

20

I don't fall into an easy sleep. Mike and Chase don't seem to, either, but I can't be sure their whispering is out of nervousness over the future, or excitement over being together. I envy that.

As they whisper I think of what Michelle said. Not just the potential of using our evidence, but the rest, all the points about who I was and who I could still be. That's the shit about addiction. You spend so much time thinking about scoring, and then being high, that it's all moment-to-moment. I don't think about past or future, only the present.

Beyond that, even in the centers, getting clean is such a process of *me, me, me* thinking, that I've barely taken into account all the others who I've hurt, and all the others who are also willing to help. It's not that I haven't been asked to, it's just, like with everything else, I haven't succeeded. I guess I've never fully realized the depths of all this, my self-loathing and inability to see what's right in front of me. It's scary how far I've gone. But as I toss and turn, I'm holding onto Chase's words, and Mike's words, and Michelle's. They've got their shit a bit more together, and I'm glad they want to help.

Morning breaks and I'm still awake, staring at the door and the light shining through. I may have drifted off, but Chase and Mike are snoring away behind me. I sit up and peer out the space in the door and can see inside Michelle's home. Her parents are up, her dad in a shirt and tie, holding a coffee mug and watching the TV. Her mom's making lunch, and the two seem to speak back and forth a bit. Then her dad sets his mug down and kisses her on the top of the head. He trails a hand along her cheek and then disappears. Her mom tilts her head in the direction he's gone, and this moment fills me with more warmth than the sun's rays.

There's a goal here. One I can see. One that is tangible. My parents may behave the same way, but I just never notice. I see distraught faces, hopeful smiles, and two adults who have no clue how the fuck this all happened. I can change that, though. And maybe in the process, provide a way for others not to get lost. Because I guarantee if we found Rashad or any of the others who've gotten out, they would be shells of human beings, and isn't that what we were before?

I lean my head against the door and feel the warmth of the wood and drift off with the hope that today will provide a route back to where I'm supposed to be.

The door flies open and I fall forward.

"Kenny!" Michelle yells above me.

I pull myself up and rub my face. "Sorry, must have fallen asleep leaning against it."

Michelle has donuts, and they teeter on the plate she's holding when she squats down to take a look at me.

She rubs my hair with her free hand. "What am I going to do with you?"

"I don't care what you do with Kenny," Mike says, "but could I get one of those?"

I turn to him in mock horror.

"Relax, Kenny. I'll share my donuts with you once we're free."

"Don't agree to that," Chase says. "This boy never shares his food."

"All right, all right, there's enough for everyone." Michelle puts the plate down in our now usual spot on the mower.

"You all want coffee?" she asks.

"Are you a mind reader or an angel?" Chase asks.

"A little bit of both. I'll be right back."

"Hold up," I say. "Let me help."

Michelle turns back, and then looks around the yard. I look, too. There's nothing but us and fence. "Fine. But stay toward the back of the house. Don't get near the front window."

I follow her up the back steps to the kitchen and realize how wobbly the steps are.

"Dad's going to fix those. Or so he says."

We enter the house and the kitchen is exactly how I remember it, and not just the layout. The island, the fridge, the sink, nothing has changed, and it's due. Michelle doesn't comment about this, but rather, keeps her head down and grabs a tray for the coffee and condiments.

The walls are a faded yellow above the same blue carpet, which desperately needs to be replaced. As does the living room set. My family's broke as hell, so I'm not judging, but it's clear to me that sacrifices have been made, either out of necessity or for security. And here I stand, worth what it would cost to spruce things up.

"Let me take it." I pick up the tray and the mugs clatter together.

"Don't drop it. I really don't want to have to explain why there are shattered mugs out back."

"I'm fine," I say, as I almost trip over the threshold to the back door. Michelle takes the coffee pot off the tray, and we descend.

"Put it on the table, we're fine now. Everyone's gone."

I do as I'm told and Mike and Chase emerge from the shed, sniffing the air like dogs. We settle around the coffee and Chase puts in far too much sugar, but no one comments about it. The caffeine is exactly what I needed, because three sips in and I feel like my brain has been recharged.

"So, I emailed a few groups in the area, as well as the ACLU," Michelle says.

"What did you say?" I ask.

"I was careful about wording things with the local groups—lawyers, addiction specialists, etcetera—but I sent some cropped video to the ACLU."

"What did you send?" Mike asks.

Michelle sips her coffee. "You remember Hobson?"

We all nod.

"Okay, I figured you would. Well, you two had quite the encounter with him. He basically laid out all the things you were saying, Kenny. How you're dispensable and so on." Michelle shakes her head. "I don't know how you dealt with it. That was chilling. Even now, I can hear his voice and it gives me goose bumps."

"He's not unique, though," I say. "I mean, yeah, for the facility, that was a perfect choice to show what the program's all about. But a lot of the treatment centers are like that, too. They act like they care when you're signing papers with your parents, but once treatment begins, they tear you down every way they can."

"Just to build you back up," Chase says.

"And watch you fall," Mike finishes.

"Business as usual." We clink our mugs together. Michelle does not find this amusing.

"It's ridiculous, but at least you understand. I can't imagine if this new program is all some addict knows."

"Probably the best patient, ever. Too stupid to think for themselves," Mike says.

"Or too scared," Chase says.

We're quiet for a moment and then I ask, "Has anyone replied?"

"Not yet, but it's still early, so we'll give it time." She sets down her mug. "In the meantime, I was thinking that I could get measurements from all of you and run to Goodwill. At least that way you won't look like my grandpa."

Mike and Chase laugh at this, but I hate the idea of her spending any money on us. I pull out what's left from the old man's stash and place it on the table. Mike and Chase do the same. Michelle counts it. "This should do."

"Anything you want us to do while you're out?" I ask. "We could pull weeds or paint something."

Michelle waves my words away. "No. Rest. Get well. Don't go score. Don't let the cops pick you up."

Chase leans in. "Michelle, what you're taking on is huge. Is this really something you want to do, because we can get out of the way. I know some hiding spots. We can go there."

I can't help but wonder who this *we* is.

"Stop with that. I want to help. I couldn't save my cousin, and Kenny didn't just choose here for no reason. There's still sense left in that head. If I can get any one of these groups to help, I'm sure they can grant you some sort of amnesty, and you won't have to live in my shed." She smiles. "What the government is doing is wrong, regardless of the intent. They've gone too far, and so let's help them find a solution that doesn't ruin people."

***

We spend the rest of the morning in the sun, sitting on the patio, relaxing on this Friday afternoon. I only know it's Friday because Michelle told us Goodwill has deals today, so our money will stretch even further. As much as I was glad to hear that, I still feel so much guilt. I know Michelle would tell me to stop and that if I really want to absolve myself, all I need to do is stay clean.

I grab the tray, mugs and condiments when we're done, clean up and then put everything away before Michelle returns.

"Kenny, hey, on a scale of one to ten, where you at?" Chase asks, and there's no malice in his voice. It feels like he and Mike just had this conversation and they want to bring me in.

"I'm at like a five. Better than yesterday, but I'll bet it picks up as it gets closer to evening."

"Yeah, that makes sense. Friday night, action's out there."

"What about the two of you?"

"About the same. Right, Mike?"

Mike gives a thumbs up.

"Right, but I meant like, what about the two of you, if nothing happens with Michelle's emails? If it gets too difficult to stay here past the weekend? You said you know a place. What's your plan B?"

Chase says, "I'm glad you asked, honestly. We're down for sticking around and being part of supplying evidence, but only for so long. She's got it all downloaded, so maybe that's enough."

"Okay, so cut to the chase. No pun intended."

Chase shakes his head. "Right. We can hide out. We're both good at finding spots, like the old man's."

"But what about recovery?"

Chase rubs a hand over his face. "We'll have to go to meetings, but that'll be tough if they're still on the hunt for us. So, we'll just have to touch base, check the news. Day-by-day it."

"That's a shitty plan."

"That's why it's plan B. Plan A is to see this through, so long that it doesn't jeopardize Michelle's life. Shit, in a month, she's off to school. How long does something like what she's thinking take? And can she really keep us a secret that long? What happens when one of the neighborhood kids spots us, or we leave shit in the shed by accident?"

"I've been thinking the same. Okay, so, a week, tops, and if she hasn't made any headway, we'll figure out how to stay connected with her, but also get out of her hair."

"That cool, Mike?" Chase asks.

"Yeah, but Kenny, you make it sound like you're not coming with us."

"I'd be a third wheel and all. You two are good together. I don't want to mess that up."

Mike gets up from his chair. "After what we've been through? Hell, no. You're with us, now." He kisses Chase's head. "We won't get frisky in front of you if that's what you're worried about."

"Please. People happy, in love, that doesn't bother me."

"All right. Put your hand in, like we're some team or shit."

We pile our hands on top of each other. Then I ask, "What do we say?"

"Fuck heroin?"

We laugh at Chase's suggestion, but go with it, and just as our cheer is dying out, Michelle returns.

"Fashion show, time!" she calls and sets down three bags. Each has two outfits, complete with sneakers and new socks. No underwear.

We change on the spot, because we can't contain ourselves, and Michelle cracks up. The clothes smell like starch and faintly like whomever else used to own them, but they're the right size, and I'm thrilled with a pair of jeans and a green T-shirt that says "Kiss Me I'm Irish," even though I'm not.

Mike and Chase have similar outfits. T-shirts and jeans. Michelle picked up shorts for us as well, and a long-sleeve T, too.

We step into our kicks and they're dirty and totally off-brand, but we pretend like we're fashion models and spin and turn on the back patio. Michelle claps and pretends to have a camera on us. "Yes, more spinning. Love the camera. Be the camera."

I look her dead in the face and blow a kiss. Surprisingly, she blushes.

Then Chase goes off script and starts doing cartwheels off to the side yard. Mike follows him, but true to his word about his sub-par athletics, falls into a heap. They look at me and chant, "Kenny! Kenny! Kenny!"

I know there's no way in hell I'll be able to do this, but I'll give it a go. I run, hit the grass and plant my hand. As I do, I see Mike and Chase turn from me, and look toward something at the front of the house. I focus on my actions, so I don't break my arm, and complete my turn. I land with both feet on the ground and do not fall. But when I look up, Mike and Chase are on their feet as well. Michelle has come to my side.

"Kenny?" Mom says.

I will my body to stay upright, to not pass out, to see the entire scene: my mother, and just beyond her, my parents' car, parked across the cul-de-sac, in a neighbor's driveway. The neighbors now coming out the front door to join the scene.

"Hi." My voice is not mine, but a boy's. Like one who's been caught and knows it.

"What? What are you doing here?" Mom asks. Her voice rises with the question, and it's clearly a mix of concern and confusion, with a tinge of anger.

"I can explain. But please try to stay calm."

"Calm? Kenny! You're a fugitive." She takes in Mike and Chase, now. "And so are the two of you." Her head swivels until she finds Michelle. "What is going on, Michelle?"

"Please stay calm, Mrs. Jenkins. I'll explain. Why don't we go to the back of the house?"

I see what Michelle sees, the neighbors approaching and my mother about to lose her shit. We have to contain this.

"I'm not going anywhere! I want to know what is going on."

"Denise, are you okay?" one of the neighbors asks. There's a husband and wife, it seems, and the dad already has his phone in hand.

My gut tells me to run. But I can't. My mother is here. Michelle is working to help us. There might be a way through. I turn to Chase, though. "Think about plan B."

He nods.

"Hey, aren't you the three—" the dad begins to say, but Mom cuts him off.

"Yes! They are! And that's my son." She points at me. "I'm trying to understand why they're here."

Michelle takes a step forward. "Let us explain." She looks at the dad. "I know Lexi's using and that you're trying to keep her from OD'ing, so trust me, you're going to want to hear what they have to say before you call the cops."

The dad's eyes darken and he squeezes his phone. "We're only trying to do what's best for our daughter," he says.

Now I understand. Mom's always done this, met with families whose children are addicts. Even though she's had zero success with me, somehow people seek her out. I'm still alive, so I guess that demands some respect.

"Mom. Mom, look at me."

She does, and I hold her gaze and refuse to break it.

"It's bad inside Ward. 15 The program is not what it seems. If you let us, we will show you."

"How, Kenny?"

"It's a long story, but I promise it will be worth hearing."

She looks me over and then Chase and Mike, too. The parents stare, and Michelle's running her tongue across her front teeth. "Are you clean?"

"Yes. I haven't used since I went inside."

"It's true," Michelle says. "I've been watching over them, like I did with Andrew."

His name causes the parents to recoil. I bet Andrew got their kid started.

"These three," the mom says. "They're worth sixty-grand."

The dad looks us over and Mom turns toward him. "Don't," she says. "Let's hear what they have to say. This is *my* son, and I can't give you advice about what they've seen. Think about Lexi. Your daughter deserves the best. And if our program isn't it—"

"But that kind of money could pay for whatever she needs," the mom says. "We can still hire private services before she overdoses. That's not against the law. I'm sure that kind of money could get her clean."

The dad stares at his wife, and then us again, and then he re-grips his phone. Mike squeaks.

"Please, sir. Don't do that. I know the money is enticing, and I don't blame you for wanting your daughter to receive the best care. But if you do this, you might ruin the chance for so many people to not have to endure what's going on inside our government's walls."

"Why the hell should I care about other junkies?" He turns to Michelle. "It's trash like your addict cousin that turned my daughter into what she is today."

I hold up my hands in pure surrender. "I can't argue that point, but as someone who's been through a lot of treatment, I have to ask, what are you going to do if all that money doesn't work?"

Neither answers.

"That's my point. Keeping her home might be fine, now, but what if the law is changed in six months or a year, and all addicts—not only those who have OD'd—have to go away. You'll be left with the government's help. Trust me, you don't want her to experience what we have." I point to my neck. "You see this?" I know the cut is still healing and is red and raw and obvious, so I don't wait for his answer. "They have them, too." Chase and Mike both tilt their heads back to reveal their own healing wounds. "Those are from implants. If your daughter goes in, she'll get one, too. And when she gets out...*if* she gets out, she won't be the same anymore."

"But that's the point," the dad says. "We want her changed."

"Not like this, you don't," I say.

"Why? What happened to you?" Mom asks. Her voice has been harsh, ready to spit anger or cut me down, but it softens with this question, which gives me hope. There are tears in her eyes when I look at her.

"It takes over, Mom. The implant, the chip, it's like a computer living inside you. It kills the addiction, but it also kills off who you are."

"That sounds like the kind of lie an addict would say to get out of trouble," the mom says. "Lexi sounds just like you."

"It's true, though," Michelle says. "I can show you the truth. I downloaded all the data from their chips. You can see for yourself if you just come inside."

"Yeah, right. We go inside that house and you'll knock us out or something," the dad says.

"No, that wouldn't happen. I could move my monitor to the window, though. You could watch from there." The parents frown at each other, but Mom looks intrigued. "I'm sorry, it's on my desktop, I can't just bring it out here."

The dad says something to the mom and she nods, and I feel a moment of relief. Then the dad raises his phone and punches three numbers. "Yes, I'd like to report that I've found the fugitives."

Time stops. I hear the man speaking, but the words don't register, yet the impact of them does. Both Michelle and Mike are shedding tears. Mom is staring at the grass. The mom is smirking, and Chase is waving at me. I know what he wants, just like it's clear what these parents want. I turn to him. "Plan B. Go, now."

He whispers in Mike's ear and he wipes his face. They turn to the back, and when I don't go with them, they stop. "Kenny, come on," Mike says.

I shake my head. "No. Go. Stay clean. Stay in touch with Michelle."

"Kenny, you can't—"

"I can and I am. Get the fuck out of here! Save yourself."

Mike and Chase look at me for a long moment, while the dad's voice drones on. "You're our one in ten, Kenny," Mike says. "We won't ever forget this." And then they're off, at a dead sprint through the woods.

21

The dad has ended his call, but now that Mike and Chase are sprinting, he taps his screen again to get it back. I walk over to him and snatch the phone out of his hands. I step into the road and slam his phone against the pavement. "You'll have to figure things out with only twenty-thousand." Then I sit, and the sirens are already audible.

"What are you doing?" Michelle screams at me. "Get up! Go with them!"

I shake my head and look straight forward.

She shoves me and I rock at the force. "No! You can't do this. You can't just give up. Not when you actually have a chance!"

"It's the only way," I say. "You have what we need. Mike and Chase will stay in touch, just wait."

"How does that help you?"

"It doesn't, but I'm responsible for them. I brought them here, to you. It was dangerous, but it was the right move."

Michelle squats down next to me. Her eyes are filling with tears, just like mine. "You're not in the program anymore, Kenny. You are not responsible for them and they aren't responsible for you."

"Yes, we are. That's the only good in all of this. The fact that I have people I care about. It's the only reason I haven't used. Trust me, I've wanted to score ever since we came here, but because of them and because of you, I've kept my shit together."

"Great, so now you're going to throw that all away?"

"No. A sacrifice isn't throwing things away. You know that."

She breaks at this, because she truly does understand, in so many ways. Michelle wraps me up in an enormous hug, and I let myself fall into it. Her tears pool along my neck and her sobs rattle through me. "I'm not done fighting, Kenny. Not for you, not for Mike and Chase. Not after what I've seen. This is enormous, so much bigger than addiction. I'll find an answer."

"Thank you, but please don't give up on yourself. Go to RIT. You can still help us from there, maybe even more so. Don't give up on yourself. That's one sacrifice I won't allow."

She squeezes me one last time and then abruptly walks away, tears streaming down her face, promising nothing.

The cop cars pull around the corner and the neighbors back away from me. Mom squats down. "How much of what you said is true?"

"All of it."

"Come on, Kenny. I'm your mother. I know you, and you always have a nice mix of truth with your lies."

The cops get out, guns drawn, and seem confused that there's only me sitting here. I ignore them and turn to Mom.

"Before I did drugs and I told you something, did you question it?"

"No. Why?"

"Right. Because you knew I was speaking from my heart, that I was some innocent child. I haven't lost that, Mom. I'm still him, and if you can't believe me, then believe him. Because everything we said is true. If this program continues, this country, maybe our world, will never be the same."

She opens her mouth to say something, but a police officer shoves me onto my face and handcuffs me before she has the chance.

Then it's business as usual. I'm stuffed into the back of the police car and the cops then go and talk to the neighbors and Mom. People emerge from their homes to get a look at the activity, but it's still early enough that there's not much of a crowd. Michelle hasn't come back out, and I doubt she will. I hope she's doing whatever she can to hide her computers, because I am sure they'll get confiscated before dinner.

And if that happens, will it have all been for nothing? Not with Mike and Chase free. And I know Michelle's smart enough to upload our data somewhere they won't look or can't find. Meantime, I hope the same is true for Chase and Mike. I don't want to see them ever again, on the inside.

The cops finish up their conversation, hand cards to the neighbors and to Mom. Of all the places for her to be offering advice. Is this Karma, or one of the two connections I'll never be able to sever? She looks over at the car and waves, but then falls in step with the neighbors. They chat at the end of the driveway, as the cop gets behind the wheel. He turns to get a look at me. "Damn, kid. You sure did fuck this up. Never run away that close to home." He laughs and turns around.

He follows the other cop out of the cul-de-sac, and soon we're out of the neighborhood and heading toward the city center.

"What are you charging me with?"

"That's not up to me. Way above my paygrade. The DA handles that, but we're not going before a judge."

"What? Then where are you taking me?"

"For someone smart enough to break out, you really are pretty stupid, huh? Or are you just high?"

The realization hits like a slap in the face. I'm a junkie. That is the truth of all of this. I believe that drugs are fun and because of this and all that I have done, the world only knows me as some burn out. Doesn't matter if I try to do good. Some stains don't wash clean. But the government sure can erase them.

Ward 15 looms in the distance like the decrepit school it was when I was a child. But now that I know what lies within, it's more terrifying than I ever could have imagined.

"Welcome home," the officer says, with obvious glee.

We pull into the back and I can more clearly see the cafeteria turned patient bay. No one is currently being admitted, so I'm a little confused by the amount of people out on the dock, until I see that there are four nurses, Dr. Williamson, and Hobson. Next to the nurses is a bed, and attached to it, restraints.

My heart has plummeted many times, but the sensation I feel now makes all those descents seem like mere blips. My life is about to end, and I know it. There's an irony here. My life should have ended before I got here, while in my bed. And now I'm back, only to be reborn into my death.

"Long time, no see," Hobson greets me after the cop has opened my door.

I say nothing.

He grabs my neck and twists it around, looking at the wound. I can't fight back, and not simply because I'm still handcuffed. It would be so futile.

"Well, someone's been messing around with his chip." He grips my neck and works his hand around until he finds the implant. Then he gives a good squeeze and I feel like I'm suffocating. "Still intact. Good." Hobson looks me straight in the eye. "We can pick up right where we left off. That is, after you serve your punishment."

The cop unlocks my cuffs and Hobson thanks him. Then the director leads me up the ramp to the rest of the waiting team.

Dr. Williamson steps to me and slaps me across the face. I can barely hear her when she speaks because the ringing in my head is so loud. "Don't you ever touch me, again!"

At that, the nurses each grab a limb, hoist me up, and slam me onto the bed. I don't fight, but they roughly situate the restraints around my wrists and ankles. I'm not so terrified as I am ashamed. They can do whatever they want to me, but there's nothing they can do to make me feel worse about myself than I already do.

They wheel me inside and down the hall. I stare at the lights and wait for the noise of the ward. I don't understand the restraints, beyond making a very obvious statement about their control. But the noise of the ward doesn't emerge. The elevator does, and then the nurses' faces are over me, as well as Williamson's and Hobson's.

We descend and then I am wheeled out and into the basement, the beginning of the end, and now, right back to the beginning. Instead of moving toward the cells, I'm steered toward the examination room across from the surgical suite. And as they turn the bed to wheel it in, I see someone atop the bed, under the light of the surgery room. He sees us and looks up.

Rashad does not smile, does not show anger. In fact, he doesn't show any emotion.

"Rashad!" I scream, but he must not hear me, because he doesn't react in any way.

Then I'm in the room and still strapped to the bed and totally confused. "Is that Rashad? Why is he back? Is there something wrong with his chip? His implant?"

Dr. Williamson looks down at me. "Yes."

She moves away but Hobson is still hovering over me. "Why didn't he respond? Why doesn't he know his name?"

Hobson looks genuinely confused. "Why would he? He's no longer Rashad."

It's a struggle to form the question, but I force it out. "Who is he?"

Hobson leans closer. "Like you, anyone we want him to be."

A strap is placed around my head and secured to the bed behind me. Then a neck brace, like they use for MRIs, is placed over that so I cannot move my head, neck, or shoulders. Dr. Williamson reappears, this time with a scalpel in hand. "Let's see what you've done to yourself."

The scalpel cuts like fire and I can feel blood drip along my neck.

Dr. Williamson tsks. "It's a shame. Whoever was in here had a golden opportunity. They could have removed this all and we might not be able to start over so easily. But," she holds a microchip on her fingertip, "all I need to do is give you version 2.0 and Kenny no longer exists."

The fear is overwhelming. Even if f I weren't essentially already paralyzed, I wouldn't be able to do anything. I will never know myself again. I'll have the blank expression I just saw on Rashad. A "shell of my former self" doesn't even come close to who I will be. I will cease to exist.

I shouldn't be surprised. This has been their plan all along.

"Any last words, Kenny?" Dr. Williamson asks.

I have nothing, and she smiles, then turns away. When she does, though, I hear a voice, not mine, but one that is distinct and clear, and recognizable. *Are you there?*

As ridiculous as it seems, I answer the voice coming from within my head. "Yes, Michelle, I'm here."

Good. I am, too. Don't worry about what she's about to do, I'll be here for you, Kenny. I'll get you back to yourself.

Dr. Williamson returns, this time with gloves and tools. I look at her, but speak to Michelle. "Promise?" I ask.

Promise, I hear.

***

I'm back in one of the cells. The walls are all within reach and the dampness is pervasive. I'm not sure how I got here, but I remember the conversation with Williamson, that she was replacing my chip.

Then I remember Rashad. I sit up, heart racing. I saw Rashad, and he was clearly lost. But I know who I am. I know where I am. How can this be?

Hey, you're awake.

Michelle's voice makes me jump. I look around the room, but stop, and remember that as well.

"Michelle?" I whisper.

Are you okay? That room looks like a dungeon.

"You can see what I see? Like, in real time? How?"

And hear what you hear. That doctor said I missed a golden opportunity. No, I didn't. I let her believe that. I modified the chip and hijacked their program, read the code beneath the data I pulled. It was pretty easy, but I'll tell you about it later.

As much as I love that I have this connection, I'm still freaked the fuck out. There's a voice in my head that sounds like Michelle, and probably is Michelle's. But I've done enough drugs to know that trusting the voices that emerge in your head is not the brightest idea.

"Is that really you?"

She sighs. *You've got to stop talking, Kenny, but here's proof. When you tried to kiss me that first time, you closed your eyes and ended up kissing my nose.*

I facepalm myself. It's true. She's here for me, still, which is amazing, but I have so many questions I want to ask. I think and then hold up my hands. The left is a five and the right an O.

Are you asking me about the cops?

I nod.

Oh, they came over, all right. Some detectives came and talked to your mom and the neighbors. I watched it all play out. So, by the time they got to me, I just lied. When they told me I'd been harboring criminals, I told them they were crazy, that yeah, you guys showed up on my lawn, but that was it. You'd trespassed. They wanted to know more about the data I had, but I played it off that I didn't know what the hell you guys were talking about when you said that, and I was afraid that you were high.

I give her a thumbs-up.

They'll be back though, which is why I cleaned the shed and have already wiped my computers. I'm talking to you through my phone. How fucked up is that?

I'm still trying to process the fact that I'm back on the ward, and this, what Michelle's done, is blowing my mind. I'm not sure how much more I can handle.

Don't worry, I'm recording it all. The cloud is a beautiful thing.

I mime being on a phone, and then someone taking it away.

I'll pull the SIM card if that happens.

I lean back and look up at the door. At some point, they'll be back. I don't know what they'll do or what they'll want, but it's not for me to be like this: aware, with functioning memories.

I don't know how to mime this question, so I say, "Rashad?"

Was he the kid across the hall from you? The one with the blank expression?

I nod.

Not yet.

She's answered this question already, sort of, but I feel compelled to know, so I point at my head and say, "How?"

The implant. Remember all the video I pulled earlier. It's the same, just in real time. As far as I can tell, you are all cyborgs, and that's how they want it. Your eyes let them see things they never would. Your microphones let them in on things they'd never know.

I point and stare at the camera above me.

They need to go back and review that footage. Can't listen to everyone at all times. Which is why they can tap in and out of all of you by simply switching to your profile. At least, that's my guess. They're going to love this "conversation."

"Then who am I supposed to be?"

You already know. You saw Rashad. You heard Hobson. You'll be whoever they want you to be. Play along. If they ask about this, just act like you don't know what they're talking about. So long as you just become Kenny 2.0 they won't give a shit.

It's sound advice. If I just play the part, it will buy me time. But for what? I wish I knew sign language.

You're going to be okay. We just need for you get back on the ward. Then I can gather evidence of how you're being treated, what they're actually doing to you, all of you. We'll figure it out as we go.

I hold up my palms and shrug.

It's all about exposure. I will get this info into the right hands.

I mime shooting myself in the head.

Keep your chin up, Kenny. Remember your uncle's five rules.

My eyes bug, the question obvious, I'm sure.

Michelle clears her throat. *I just spoke to Mike and Chase. That was Mike's advice to you.*

I bug, again.

Yes, Kenny. We're going to help you.

As I'm trying to figure out how to ask about Mike and Chase, the door slides open. Standing in the hall, is Hobson.

And...action! Remember, you know nothing.

Hobson squats down in front of me and I hope the placid look I'm forcing my face into is believable.

"Kenny? How are you feeling?"

I don't react, just look at him a bit more closely.

"Kenny?" Hobson says.

I sit up. "Are you talking to me, sir?"

Hobson grins. "I don't know, am I?"

"It seems that way, but why are you calling me Kenny?"

"Isn't that your name?"

I wait a beat, two. "I don't know my name."

Hobson's smile breaks his face in two. "Let's get you upstairs, Kenny. I have plans for you."

I stand and do no more. I force myself to forget everything I already know about the layout. I've been this stupid before, high as fuck, out of my mind. I can go there again. Use that.

Hobson let's out a small laugh. "I forgot. This way." He gestures for me to step out of my cell and follow him, which I do. I take my time, go slow, allow myself to be led, like a well-behaved dog on a leash. One that can't wait to tear off his master's face.

22

Before we step into the elevator, Hobson has me change. I say nothing when he says, "You get to be a blueberry again." His forehead wrinkles while I slide into the outfit and then stare straight ahead. I'm running on pure guesswork for how I'm supposed to behave, and I hope I'm not already messing up.

The elevator brings us up to the same hallway I ran from just days ago. Hobson looks, pointedly, at the door, but I keep up my dumb-as-dirt routine. He tilts his head and leads the way to my previous ward.

"You'll have about ten minutes to get settled, and then your wing has group. Okay?"

"Okay," I say and we enter.

The nurses watch me. I ignore them all, and stay on Hobson's heels. They whisper at my back, but I can't make out what they're saying

"Here you are. And this is your roommate, Rashad."

Rashad stands at his name, but stays by his bed, ramrod straight.

Hobson brings me into the room. "Rashad, this is Kenny. Can you say hello?"

Rashad reaches out to shake my hand. I take his and its cool to the touch. "Hello, Kenny," he says, pumps my hand once and then releases it. I follow his lead and stand, stupid, after. Hobson looks at us both, and I'm sure he's pleased with himself. The two patients who ignited the explosion that led to our escape are back in the same room with each other, and neither has a clue.

"Okay, then. Kenny, that's your bed. Go sit on it and wait to be called." Hobson all but pats me on the head.

I go to the bed and sit. Rashad then does the same. We both stare out into the same space between us, seeing entirely different worlds. Hobson shakes his head one last time and then leaves.

There is silence. No one on the ward is talking. No one's calling out to anyone else. I don't know who else is here, if they've released Devon and Big James and Ramirez, or if they are here, they're like Rashad is now. Like I'm supposed to be.

This is hella creepy.

Michelle's voice makes me jump again. I'll get used to it at some point, I guess. "I know," I whisper.

Rashad looks over, waits a second, and then turns back.

See! Don't talk! He's like a robot, and you're doing a good job of being like him. Keep it up.

I sit for a while, staying as perfectly still as possible, and so does Rashad. Michelle keeps reminding me to stay chill.

"Time for group," a nurse calls from the hall.

Rashad stands, turns and walks out the door. Normally, he'd be at the front. Normally, the rest of the guys who I can't see, but can hear lining up, would be talking to one another. But nothing's normal anymore.

I follow him, step into the hallway, and falter for a second, because they're all here. Ramirez and Devon and Big James. They stand at attention like the rest and stare ahead and say nothing. One of the nurses is watching me. He removes his foot from the wall behind him and starts walking toward me. I correct myself, immediately, turn away from the line and follow Rashad to the back.

The nurse follows me as I square up at the end. "You all, right, Kenny?"

I turn just my head and do not answer.

"Something happen back there? You looked confused."

"I wasn't sure which way to turn. Sorry." My voice is as flat as I can make it. The monotone unnerves me.

The nurse nods, slowly. "Okay. That makes sense. Anything else I should know?"

"No," I say and turn to face Rashad's back.

The nurse chuckles and steps back. He gestures to another nurse and the line moves forward. I step in time with the rest, keeping my eyes on Rashad's neck.

That was good, Kenny. Keep it up.

I don't nod or make any other errant move. I can't risk it.

John, the counselor, greets us, but only by saying "Welcome." He doesn't use our names and he doesn't even direct anyone to sit or pay attention. He doesn't have to. The entire group takes a seat and stares ahead at the screen in the front of the room. John's footsteps are the only noise beyond the very faint sound of breathing.

"Well, here we are, again." John shakes his head. "I mean, here we are." He stops, looks us over. "Not that it matters. You can't remember."

It's as if he's speaking to a wall. No one laughs or looks at each other, wondering what the hell his point is. They all are as quiet as house plants, and I play along.

"So, because we need this as part of your memory, I want you to watch the screen. It will give you all you need to know."

John steps away and the screen lights up. Rather, the screen darkens and the code spilling across it lights up. Because that's all there is, a website banner-like stream of code spilling across the screen. I stare for a moment, but look away, ever so slightly, so that I can see how the rest are reacting.

It's as if the most amazing footage is being shown. They are transfixed by the ones and zeros and bits of text and breaks and the rest of code language that I was too busy getting high to ever learn. I look back at the screen and it keeps coming.

Don't look away. Something's happening right now to your system. I think you're supposed to be absorbing this, like a software update. I want to download it and figure out what they're doing. This is exactly the stuff we need.

I stare, and I focus as hard as I can, so I blend, and so that Michelle gets what she needs. Then, a few minutes later, the script ends. The screen goes blank, and John says, "Thank you, everyone. You may leave."

As we sat, now we rise, and the line forms again. We file back to our rooms and we sit on our beds. And nothing else happens. There's no conversation, no talk whatsoever of addiction, of recovery. It's as if I've dropped into alien territory.

Are you okay?

I look over at Rashad before answering. I need to see what he does when I whisper again. "No."

His head moves slightly, but he does not look at me.

I don't blame you. That shit was weird. Not at all what I expected, either. I figured they'd be doing shock therapy or something. Not this. That code you just watched, it was a scripted memory. You all just experienced Ramirez have a breakthrough in his recovery. It was a tearful and heart-wrenching moment.

I whip my head back and forth.

I'm not kidding. The script has some amazing dialogue in it. They've hired a writer, I bet.

I shrug with my palms up.

My guess, they build you up like this, with these memories, and then they switch you back to human mode and you remember all this shit, so that when you go home and people ask you about what happened, you have these stories to tell. It's a really efficient model. Not genuine, but pretty damn astounding.

I don't like her appreciation for this mind-fuck, but I keep that to myself. If what she's suggesting is true, it does have a bit of credibility. If this is the second wave, they've laid a great foundation. Patients weren't allowed to call home before, and that makes complete sense now. Most were out within three months, but if all they're going to have us do is sit and read code, they could probably have us out in a day, but better to roll it out slowly, or someone, like that film crew, will start asking too many questions. None of them will have human-looking answers. Which is why they probably let them in when they did, and probably let them fuck up. Shit, we might have been set-up to escape. You need a screw up to justify tightening security.

I was always going to be a sacrifice.

Do you think they'll feed you or just insert feeding tubes?

I try not to laugh, but I'm in a weird place and the dark humor gets me. Rashad's head jerks and he stares at me. I stare back, but then remember myself and look away. He stands up.

Rashad was a tough kid, in real life, but now, with the lack of expression, his deep brown eyes are even more menacing when he squats before me and stares into my own.

I want to look away, but I know I can't. He's doing *something*, but I don't know what and I don't know why. Is he even doing this through free will? Can't be. Someone must be making him do this. Someone who's watching. Chills ride up my back and the hair on my neck stands up. Rashad notices this, and like a photographer, seems to zoom in on this very human reaction to fear.

Then, as if on command, he stands and returns to his bed. He sits and stares.

What the fuck was—

Michelle is cut off by the entrance of one of the nurses. "Kenny, come with me."

I hesitate, but then force myself to stand. Wherever I'm going, there is no choice, because even if I were to refuse, it'd blow my cover. I turn to the nurse and he steps back into the hallway.

Again, the staff whispers, but this time I hear, "Bet she left it a little off so she could tweak him."

I don't have to guess at the subjects of this.

The nurse brings me down the hall and to Medical. "Stand here," he says, and I notice there are no longer seats for the patients. He talks to a nurse behind the counter and she taps her tablet, then comes around the desk, to me.

"This way," she says and turns before I can respond, because there's no need for that anymore.

I'm brought to a curtained room and told to sit on the bed. The nurse leaves and I wonder how long the curtains will last. What's the point?

Dr. Williamson parts the curtains and enters with a tablet and a wand. She stands before me and looks me over for a moment. "Seems as if you aren't completely settled in yet."

I don't know if she's talking to me or about the chip.

"Let's take a look." She holds the wand, which is now connected to her tablet, up to my neck and presses the trigger. A shock zips through me and I jump. Williamson notices. "Did you feel that?" she asks.

Do I lie? Do I even answer? "Yes," comes out of my lips before I've even thought it through.

Williamson frowns, taps her tablet and then presses the wand to my neck. "How about now?"

The current this time, is stronger, and I cry out.

Williamson doesn't cut the source, immediately, but when she does, merely tilts her head and says, "Interesting." Then she taps her tablet again and puts the wand up to my neck. "Now?"

I brace myself, even bite down on my tongue so that I don't speak, but this current is so strong, it's as if I'm a puppet and the hand moving inside me has spread wide. My limbs shoot out and I scream. Doc removes the wand from my neck and the jarring lack of current sends me sprawling into a heap on the floor. I pant and moan and then feel the breath of her voice on my neck.

"I'm so glad that I left your pain receptors on. This is going to be a very enjoyable three months. For me, of course."

She stands and I lie on the ground for a moment, trying to think through what I should do next, because if I can feel pain, then it's fine if I take my time.

"Get up, Kenny, it wasn't that much voltage."

I pull myself together, in spite of the stinging sensation running throughout my body, and stand, but say nothing.

Dr. Williamson approaches, much in the same way Rashad did. She looks directly into my eyes, and it's so difficult not to turn away, to be human. "I don't know, however, why you seem to be talking to yourself. Is there something you need to tell me, Kenny?"

The question brings the beginning of a smile to my lips. One I suppress. I've been asked this question countless times, and can't remember when I've ever offered something worthwhile, or something true.

"No," I say, because *yes* and *no* seem like acceptable answers around here.

"Are you sure? Because if you're remembering anything, and you're trying to talk your way through what those memories are, you can tell me. I can fix that."

I'm sure she can *fix* anything that's *wrong* with me. It's what happens after that I'm worried about. Maybe the cure can be worse than the disease.

I stare ahead and say nothing.

She extends a hand to my neck and traces circles around my wound. Like before, my skin prickles with goose bumps. "Look at that. Pleasure and pain all wrapped up into one."

She could not have summarized this situation any better.

"That's all for now, Kenny."

She leaves and another nurse comes in and escorts me out. I have no idea how long I've been gone, but Rashad is seated as he was when I left. I mirror him, while the current continues to dissipate throughout me. I didn't hear Michelle's voice during that session with Williamson, and I worry that whatever the doctor did has severed that communication.

Then I hear crying. Soft, muffled, but distinct.

I dare whisper, "Michelle?"

Sorry. Sorry. I'm trying not to, but what the fuck was that? Are you okay?

"Fine." I fear more than one or two-word sentences.

That's bullshit. If you could talk, like really talk to me, would you say you're fine?

I shake my head.

Okay, okay, that makes more sense. We have to keep that from happening again. Well, as much as possible. That's the one you drugged, right?"

I nod.

Well, I don't completely blame her, but I also don't agree with the situation she put you in. So...shit, I don't know. The cops have been back and my parents keep asking what the real story is, and I'm afraid that we're not going to make it through. I'm afraid that I've taken on more than I can handle.

This isn't her fault, and I hate hearing the fear and desperation in her voice, but she's also my only hope. I can't just say, *no worries. See you in a few months.* Because I won't. Without her, they'll figure out something's up. Williamson is just too pissed right now to see it. But she will. And then? Then I'll become one of them. I've done that once, been the addict who belongs here, but not again. My life still matters.

There's more crying and I wish I could say something else, help her through this, somehow, but I can't, and then a nurse yells from the hall, "Lunch!" and Rashad stands. I do the same. Michelle continues to cry inside my head and the door opens, and I have no idea what to expect.

23

At lunch, once the nurses have receded to their wall to talk, I wait for someone else to break, to start talking, to make any gesture that lets me know I'm not the only one. No one does.

We've all been served the exact same meal: sandwich, apple, milk. And everyone eats in exactly the same manner. Two bites of sandwich, followed by a sip of milk. The apple is being saved for last. I stare at Big James, because this meal has to be killing him, but he nibbles like a child and sets his sandwich down and sips his milk like the rest, all while staring straight ahead.

The apple is no longer ripe. I almost spit it out at the first bite, but no one else does, so I stomach it out, and swallow the entire, rotted piece of fruit.

A nurse yells, "Trays!" and everyone stands and moves into a line so that we can calmly and efficiently deposit our trays.

Then we line up by groups and our nurse stands at the front like some camp counselor. He says, "Blue" and we move, like soldiers, like a train, straight back to the group room. Normally, people would be bitching. What about our break? What about art therapy? What about anything but more group? But no one is here anymore. No one remembers. It's just me, and we file into group and we sit and John says something and then we stare at a screen, and the code scrolls, and in a short while I'm back in my room staring at nothing.

I'd literally kill for heroin right now. The boredom is already stronger than my fear, and I simply cannot deal with the utter silence, the lack of real communication. Thank God Michelle comes back.

So, that was a seminar on how to reintegrate into society once you've made your way to a sober life.

I nod.

Exactly. It was very dry, and so straightforward. Guess what you do? You don't use drugs and your life is perfect, again. Huh? Guess that would mean it was perfect before. They'd better work on that. Anyway, sorry about those tears. I'm okay now.

"It's fine." I spy on Rashad again, just to be sure. I don't need his creepy, lizard like stare down. He's as placid as I've come to expect.

163

I think having to hold all that in is going to be tough, but I'm making connections. People have gotten back to me. Obviously, they want to know more, and I'm promising them I will have it, but I just don't know how long until I do.

"What do you need?"

Why? Do you think you could risk going off script to make something happen? Like a glitch or something?

I shrug.

That's actually a really good idea. Williamson already thinks something's up. Maybe Hobson does, too. If you simply broke into like normal Kenny, I think they'd panic. And then? Well, then they'd investigate, wouldn't they? And that would mean? That would mean opening up the can of worms, your neck.

There's a pause and I am thankful that Michelle is so smart and is also so comfortable spending so much time in her own head. We can't dialogue about this, but she's doing an excellent job of inserting the points I would make.

I don't want you in there any longer than you have to be, but at least you're mostly fine. Aside from Williamson and her wand, they're feeding you and giving you a place to stay. Yeah, it's more like prison than therapy, so that's not cool, but I'm not sure what I have is enough to demonstrate some real transgression.

"Simple terms."

We need the shit to hit the fan, somehow, and it can't be through you blowing your cover. They have to show their hand.

I shrug, again.

I have no idea. But I'll be watching if they do.

There's some comfort in this, and she's right, I am okay. I'm not out in the streets, I'm not currently using. I've been clean for a couple weeks now, and that is a win. Worth the cost? I have no idea.

"Mike and Chase?"

Rashad's head swivels at that, and he stares at me for a moment, but does not get all up in my face.

They're in an old farmhouse. A place Chase knew. They're clean, so they tell me. Scared for you, but seem to be okay for now.

For now. How long does *for now* last?

The door opens and Hobson steps into the room. His shoes crack against the floor in a way that makes me feel as if he's here with a purpose, not just a check in. He looks at me and then Rashad and then sits next to him, on the bed. Hobson stares at the floor for a moment, and if he were sitting more erect, would appear exactly as the rest of us do. But he sighs, a very non-robotic emotion, and then he runs his hand through his hair.

"This program is the future, Kenny. You probably cannot understand that, but some day you will, and some day you will thank us for eradicating addiction and the rest of the maladies that plague us." Hobson looks at me, and I don't know what he's looking for. What type of reaction does this warrant?

"Population growth is out of control. Immigration is only going to increase as global warming suffocates us. We must have a society that can stand on its own two feet and be a productive powerful force in the decades to come. We cannot do that now, not with the deplorable situation our country is in. And it is my job to make sure we get it right." He leans forward on his elbows. "We start with the disposable and we make our way up the ladder. Right to the very top." He stares straight at me. "And then we are unstoppable."

"You're fucking sick, that's what you are." The words spill out, not because I want them to, not because I want to blow my cover, but because I'm still human and have a soul and am not worse than these cyborgs around me. I am not like this man.

Hobson's smile starts out as a surprised purse of the lips, which draws quickly up and ragged. "I knew it! There was something off, but I couldn't be positive. Williamson screwed up because she's taking this personal. The fact that you bested her has interfered with her ability to do her job!" He punches his hand as if this point is driving home an argument he's been trying to win for years.

But I don't really care about that, about them. What the hell is going to happen to me now?

Just keep your eyes open, Kenny.

Hobson turns to Rashad. "Rashad, I need you to exit recovery mode."

Rashad says nothing, but a flicker sparks in his eyes.

"Now, enter protective mode."

Again, a flicker, but along with that, Rashad's shoulders pin back, and if possible, his expression deadens even more.

Hobson now looks at me, "Well, Kenny, let's see what works and what doesn't." He pauses and then says, "Kenny, exit recovery mode."

I look away so he can't see the lack of flicker in my eyes, which, in itself might be all that he needs to see.

"Kenny, enter protective mode."

I have a choice here. I could play along, string out Hobson's curiosity, maybe buy myself more time. But for what? The result of whatever's about to happen in this room is me on a table with Williamson opening my neck. Might as well see if I can get the monster to lift the veil even more.

"Can't do that, Hobson," I say.

"Excuse me?"

I look at him now and he's more confused than concerned. "You heard me. I don't work like the rest of these, whatever you've turned them into."

"That's obvious," he says.

"Yeah, it is. But answer me this, before Rashad does whatever it is you've programmed him to do."

Hobson smirks and waits for my question.

"Was any of it real or was it all a setup? Because the one in ten piece, that actually helped. It felt different to be connected, to need others and for them to need you."

"Glad you enjoyed it, but it was a smokescreen. You addicts take too long to get your lives together. And some of you never do. You're fundamentally broken, because of the drugs or your backgrounds, I don't know. I don't care, though. We need a fix, not a shred of hope."

"And someday, you need soldiers. You need an unflinching army. And you need the public to believe in it, in us, not simply to place our faith in machines, because they could always revolt."

"I think maybe you've watched too much Sci-Fi, but you're not that far off. This is the new horizon. It's too bad that you're too weak to be a part of it."

"How's that?" I say.

Hobson turns to Rashad. "Rashad, read target at three meters left."

Rashad's head turns and the flicker in his eyes is now a roaring inferno.

"Voice activation or manual directives, for now," Hobson says. "Soon, it will be algorithms. Soon they will run on their own."

This idea, even more than the threat of Rashad, is terrifying.

"Rashad, enter attack mode."

Rashad rises, fists clenched, face blank. This is going to hurt like hell.

He swings, but I manage to duck the first punch. The second, however, gets me in the temple. Stars pop and I stagger back. Rashad advances and I know there's no way to match him. I have to get dirty.

I roll just as he's about to lunge and he trips over me and faceplants into the floor. Most people would need a minute to recover from that, but Rashad rolls over and pops up. There is an enormous egg on his forehead, though, growing by the minute.

The bed is at my side and I reach down and pull the blanket off. Rashad comes at me, again, and this time, I toss the blanket over his head. He tears at it, but that provides me all the time I need to squat down and grab his ankles. Then I lift and his head smacks into the floor.

He doesn't pop up this time, but he's down, not out. Rashad's eyes roll, but I know it's only a matter of time before they get fixed on a new target. So does Hobson, because he's on his feet now, yelling. "Rashad! Eliminate!"

Rashad's eyes become fixed again, and I don't know what my next move is. I've twice taken him out at the legs. He won't let that happen again, and I'm not going to be able to match him, toe-to-toe, especially not with Hobson screaming for him to eliminate me.

Go for his neck. It's your only chance.

Michelle's voice is like my own directive. I don't question, I dive, and plant my weight on top of Rashad before he's had a chance to get up. I straddle his arms and start pounding on his neck, right where the chip lies.

Hobson's screaming above us, but I ignore him and go a step further. I squeeze Rashad's neck and see the square beneath his skin. A thought enters, and I want to dismiss it, but I know this is it. This is my only chance. If I don't win, I die. Yet, if I do win, I might still die, just a slower and unconscious death.

Rashad looks at me for a moment, and there's a moment of recognition, I think. So much so that I almost let up on my squeezing. But then his eyes flare again, and I have no choice.

I bite his neck and grind my teeth down until I can feel the metal beneath. His blood is filling my mouth and I am disgusted, but I push through it, and chew. The edge of the chip catches beneath my tooth, and like a rat, I gnaw until both teeth are around the source of all this bullshit.

And then, when my teeth are touching, with the chip between their grasp, I rear my head back and Rashad's flesh tears away.

The force tosses me off him and into the bed frame. I sit for a second, with the chip between my teeth, my face and chest covered in blood, and I stare at Hobson, who has sat down, his skin so white I bet he's close to passing out.

Rashad stirs and then sits up. It's as if he's coming back to life with some help from Narcan. He looks around, sees Hobson, then feels his neck, which is spilling a steady trickle of blood. Then he looks right at me. "Kenny?"

I can't speak with this piece of him in my mouth, so I spit it into my hand. "Hey, Rashad."

"The fuck is going on?" he asks.

And for a moment, I feel good, not because I've bitten through Rashad's neck like some zombie, but because he's back. I can hear all I need to know in his voice. *This* is Rashad.

But the moment is fleeting, because a team of nurses storm in, along with Williamson.

"Give me the chip," she demands.

I separate the chip from Rashad's skin and place it in my palm. "This?" I say.

"Yes. Now!"

But at this point I know I'm done, that Rashad is done, that I'll never hear Michelle's voice again. So fuck it. As I've done so many times in my life, I swallow the pill that will kill me. The chip scratches my throat while it passes down, and I smile, in spite of the pain.

24

Williamson slaps me hard enough to knock me to the ground, and I know she wants to do more. Her eyes burn as if she has her own chip implanted.

"You stupid, piece of shit, junkie!" Williamson clenches her fists. "It's fine, though, we'll get that chip and we'll replace your entire system. No shortcuts this time."

"Kenny!" Rashad yells. Two nurses pull him off the floor. Hobson looks on, still horrified.

"Rashad, you'll be okay." I don't know why I say this, because I know it's a lie, and I really don't want to lie to him.

"But what's going on? Why are we in your room? And where's Mike?"

He clearly has no memory of anything beyond our lunchroom scene. "Don't worry. He's all right."

"That's right, calm him down," Williamson says to me. "It's the last useful thing you'll ever remember doing."

Two nurses stand me up and I am now level with Rashad. He sees something in me, because his face jumps and his hand goes to his neck. "Kenny? You're covered in blood. Is that mine?" As he speaks, his head lists, as if he's about to be sick.

"Rashad, it's all right. Don't worry, you'll be fine soon."

Rashad's eyes pop open and he stomps his feet. "Fuck, no! Kenny! The chip is gone. I feel amazing. What did you do?"

Dr. Williamson turns away from us and steps out into the hall. She returns almost immediately with a syringe.

Tell him everything. Now!

"It's all a scam, Rashad. They aren't making us better, here. They're just taking control of our bodies. That chip wasn't helping you, so it had to come out."

His face twitches at the news, clearly struggling to absorb this. "But I was almost out, and then you and me, we got into it?"

"Yeah, but that's not your fault. That was *them*." I look over at Hobson, who's regained his color. Williamson advances on Rashad, cutting straight through our conversation. "And she's going to knock you out and you'll never remember it, but I'm going to tell you, anyway. You're a good person, Rashad. You just got caught up at the wrong place at the wrong time. I'm sorry."

Dr. Williamson steps out of the way, the syringe now empty, and Rashad's head is hanging so heavily that his chin is touching his chest. She glares at me. "You should have saved your breath. Once I get him operable, I'll have him pick up where he left off."

"Why? Why not just kill the both of us?"

"You'd like that, wouldn't you?" Dr. Williamson steps closer, enough that I can see the bags under her eyes and the way she's tried to cover up a scar beneath her lip with makeup. "You'd like the easy way out. Don't want to fight through your problems. That's the same thinking that got you into drugs, which produced the same kind of behavior that turned you into an addict."

Whatever you do, don't turn away from her.

I appreciate Michelle's support, but at this point, she has to know that we're completely fucked.

"So you say. But why should I believe one word? For all I know you're not even a doctor, but some whacked out engineer that the government has brought on to be their mad scientist."

Williamson gets closer to me and laughs, something deep from within and wet-sounding. "I can promise you, Kenneth, that I am, indeed, a doctor. I've lived and breathed addiction and recovery as my life's work. So has Hobson. You can project onto us all you want, but that does not change the fact that you are an addict. That does not change the fact that no one can successfully treat this new wave of addiction. That does not change the fact that this program, this technology, was going to be put into place one way or another. Like you said to Rashad, *wrong place, wrong time.* I'd counter that for you, rather than being dead, you were at the right place at the right time."

"Whatever helps you sleep at night, *doctor.* But you should know this, before you put me under. I've been clean for a couple weeks now. And, yeah, I'd still like to use, but that won't ever go away, so no need to sweat that. If I just had a support system, like the concept you had in place—the smokescreen, as Hobson called it—then I might have stayed clean. I'll never know, now."

"You've had plenty of chances and so much support, but you've pissed away all those opportunities. You are no different than every addict I have ever known, constantly lying to yourself and others about the situation at hand. You somehow, even in this moment, believe that you can talk your way out of things. No. No longer. We are going to make use of your life, yet. You will have value to this society."

I say nothing to this, because there's a lot of truth wrapped up in what she just said, and mixed in with that is a moment of clarity. "Who was your addict?"

"How dare you!" Williamson's words sound like a curse.

"Tell me."

Hobson has stepped forward, and he's placed a hand on her shoulder. He whispers and she nods, but then brushes him off and squares to me.

"Not that you deserve to know, but my son. I was killing myself at my work, making breakthroughs, connecting artificial limbs to nerves, but I was away from home for too long, or not paying attention when I was there. My boy slipped into a crowd, and I didn't know until it was too late. And then all the recovery centers, all my connections proved to be useless. So, what good was any of it? What was the point?"

"If you couldn't save him, why bother saving anyone else?"

"You'll be as close to saved as anyone like you deserves to be."

"But I'm like your son. Would you say that about him?"

This time she punches instead of slaps. When my head straightens, she grabs my ears. Her forehead is against mine when she speaks.

"Don't ever compare yourself to my Daniel. If not for him, you'd be dead. I am saving you, and all the others like you."

"No, you're not. And some day the world will know what you've done, and you'll find out what it's like to live in a cell of your own."

"I'll be given the Nobel Prize. My image will be everywhere. I am the modern day Curie!"

Hobson's eyes widen at this, and I wonder if he knew how she sees herself. I've met egomaniacs like Williamson so many times. Both doctors and dealers with god complexes. If the implants go well, will they chip people for this attitude?

"So, what now?" I ask, done with wanting any more answers. Done with all of this.

"Like I said, surgery." Williamson turns and nods to the nurses, who march Rashad out, into the hall. My nurses bring me out after him, and there are two beds already there. Rashad is placed on one, and I am placed on another. The nurses do not restrain Rashad, but they affix mine with a bit of glee.

We're wheeled down the hall and to the elevator, and in no time, we are in the basement, back in the operating suite. Nurses swab Rashad's neck and insert an IV. I wait for my own to do the same for me, but they stand by, idly, while Williamson scrubs and then gets her surgical mask and gloves on.

"Cut off his shirt," she says, and my nurses spring to life and cut away my clothing. Sadly, this isn't the first time nurses have had to cut off my clothes, but this is the first time I've witnessed it.

Doc then squirts cold gel onto my belly and places the 3D ultrasound wand atop it. My intestines appear on the screen, and Doc follows the twisting line up to my stomach, where, practically shining bright, is Rashad's chip.

"Clean him off," Williamson says and the nurses follow orders. In a moment I am clean and Doc hovers over me with a scalpel.

"Hey, aren't you going to knock me out?"

"No, Kenny." Her smile is visible through the mask. "I want you wide awake. I want you to feel what it's like to have your stomach ripped open, and then experience the transformation with your new implant. I want you to feel every moment of pain, just like the pain you have caused all the people who love you."

She's not joking. This is not some idle threat she's using to make me comply. Williamson is going to torture me. I'd like to think this will provide Michelle with some great evidence, but I'd have to be awake for that, eyes open. The pain will undo me, I'm certain.

"Michelle?" I say.

Kenny. The tears are obvious in her voice.

Dr. Williamson looks around, as if I'm talking to one of the nurses.

"I just wanted to say, thank you. You didn't have to do anything that you did, and I hope whatever you get from here on out is enough. Probably not for me, but maybe for Rashad. Definitely for Mike and Chase."

Dr. Williamson's head snaps around at this.

I'm not finished, Kenny. Don't give up, yet.

I don't know how that's possible, but part of what Doc said, the truth, is that at some point I did give up, and then just gave in to my addict. And I've kept doing that over and over. Some of it is out of my control, but not all. There's still a human being in here, not just a shell with an addict living inside. Doc wants to eradicate that addict, but keep the shell. I just wish I could keep the me that is fully back to life in place. But a wish at this point is as good as dead.

"Okay, I promise. Thank you, Michelle."

"Who are you talking to, Kenny?" Williamson demands.

"Just a voice in my head. I'm sure your son had those, too."

"How dare you!" Doc plunges the scalpel into my side, and despite every part of me screaming not to look, I prop myself up and look at what she has done. The scalpel juts out just beneath my ribs.

"Is that all you got? Come on, if you're going to perform this surgery, against my will, without anesthesia, then get on with it."

"You don't tell me what to do. I'll do the surgery at my pace. Maybe you'll live, maybe you'll die. Maybe even after you're dead, I'll bring you back. Don't think I haven't worked on that experiment."

I know without knowing that pissing off Doc will be my salvation. After death, possibly. But I will push her into her own corner and Michelle can pull the trap door.

"You can do all you want to me. Cut me into little pieces; kill me, and bring me back; turn me into a cyborg zombie, if that's what you want." Every word causes the blade to wobble and my skin to burn, but it's worth it. "But nothing you do will bring Daniel back."

Doc's eyes flare open, and her arms jerks, and I feel the white-hot pain of the scalpel passing deeper into me. I force a laugh and stare down at the hole that has now opened in my side, the one with Doc's hand inside. I laugh in spite of the disturbing sensation of her hand wriggling within my stomach.

She holds up Rashad's chip, and her arm is covered in blood, my blood, which I can now feel spilling out of me.

"No, it won't bring Daniel back. But you and I both know that revenge is a sweet second place."

I stare and my head swims, but I keep myself upright, looking at her. "Go, ahead, then, Get your revenge."

Doc walks up to my neck and opens it up with the scalpel. "Don't worry, I will." She hooks two fingers inside me and starts tugging. The implant tears away. It feels like a giant sliver being removed, and a moment later, she holds it before me, this jellyfish-like entity that has been living inside me, and from what I can feel, is still attached.

"Time for Kenny, 2.0." She tosses the implant onto my chest and is about to say something more when Hobson runs into the room.

He doesn't look at me, just Doc. "Something's wrong. We have to go."

"What?" Doc looks like she could plunge the scalpel into Hobson. I hold onto my neck and side and apply as much pressure as I can. The room is dimming.

"We have to go! The system's been hacked! They're coming for us!"

As if in reply to what would have to be Doc's question, a flood of patients appears out in the hall. I see Big James and Ramirez and Devon, and what seems like the rest of the ward. Their eyes are wide open and searching. One sees me and screams, "Kenny!"

They all turn, as one, and scream, "Kenny!"

Then they rush the surgical suite but not before Doc locks it. "What have you done?" she asks Hobson, but I laugh, because I know what neither of them do.

The patients pound on the door and the windows. The nurses pack into a corner out of fear. It's only a matter of time before they break it all down, and then what?

"What did you do, Kenny?" Doc is shaking me now, helping me keep my eyes open.

"Not me, but through me."

Doc's forehead wrinkles.

"We are the one in ten, Doc. The power is in the group, the strength in numbers. But you already knew that."

She bends over me and screams, "How?" just as the glass around us shatters, and my vision slips from focused, to blurry, to sleep.

25

My eyes open to a wave of activity around me. There are cops and patients everywhere, but there's also an EMT in my face, yelling, "Kenny! Kenny, stay with me!"

I've been here before, but not exactly here. He's not administering Narcan, because I'm not using. But I am dying. That's one of those other secrets no one tells you, that when you're using, you know you're killing yourself, you know you're dying. But it doesn't matter. Nothing matters but scoring and getting high.

Not now, though. Now, I'm dying, but I want to live. For the first time in years I want to capital L, live.

I force my eyes open and look around. The cops are herding patients, who are not fighting, just standing around, looking shocked. Big James stares at me. "Kenny!"

He's pulled away before I can respond, but he knew me, and that's important.

"Good, Kenny," the EMT says. "Stay with me. You've lost a lot of blood but I'm giving you some now and you have emergency coagulant on your wounds. They were clean cuts, easy to patch, so you've stopped bleeding. You're going to make it."

The crook of my arm has an IV, and attached to it is a bag of blood, that is running into me, keeping me alive. The irony is not lost, even in this moment.

I turn and see that Rashad and his bed are gone. "Where?" I ask, and my voice is weak.

The EMT looks at the space. "The other guy? He's fine, just seems to have been sedated." He pauses. "Not like you, Kenny. That doctor, she was a butcher."

I see Williamson's face and can hear her voice asking me *How?* but I don't have that answer. So, I ask the EMT. "How?"

"How? As in, how did we know to come here?"

I nod, and he runs a quick check of my vitals and then pulls his phone out of his pocket, taps around and then hands it to me. I click the link, and the room is whole, un-shattered. Doc is standing over me, and she's just pulled out the chip. The picture dims, but then comes back, and the implant is pulled from my neck, followed by the conversation I had with Doc before I passed out. She screams *How?* and it goes black, but audio remains. There's shattering glass and the sound of walkie talkies and police announcing their arrival.

The EMT puts the phone down so he can have a look at my face. "Good, the color's coming back."

"I don't understand," I say.

"That makes two of us, but based on what went out with the video and what we've been told, you had some sort of implant in you. Does that make sense?"

I nod.

"Right, well, someone hacked it, and livestreamed the operation that doctor was performing. She, uh, she then called the police and told them where to watch the link and I guess she also tagged all these human rights groups and their members shared it, and we all converged, here, to find that it wasn't some hoax."

As difficult as it is to think right now, I say, "Michelle."

"Who's Michelle?"

For a moment, I wait for her voice, but I know that's impossible. "She saved me. She's the one who hacked it."

The EMT nods. "Well, then you owe her, because you're alive, Kenny. You're going to need surgery to patch you up, but your vitals are good, you're going to make it."

The last time I was face-to-face with an EMT he was bringing me around with Narcan, and the look in his eyes was the exact opposite of what I'm seeing now: concern, empathy, compassion. They flood this man's face, and maybe it's the difference between the two men, or the situation, itself. I don't know, but it's a sight I appreciate seeing.

"Okay, we need to get you to the hospital. Ready?"

"Yes," I say, and the EMT motions to his partner, who seems to be attending to a nurse with a nasty cut. Probably from the glass. I wonder how Williamson fared, whether she's shredded. I hope not. She deserves some-

thing slower, more painful. Or, maybe not. Her life seems to be its own form
of punishment.

They wheel me into the hall and the scene is surreal. I wish I were still
recording, because this would be worth seeing for everyone who has a child
in here.

Cops are asking everyone what happened, and they're all talking about
their addiction, and their failed recoveries, and what they thought this place
was, and what it turned out to be. Then someone whispers, "Is that him?"
Someone else yells, "It's Kenny!" Then the sea of cops and patients parts, and
they wheel me through. The patients clap and touch my bed, and my shoulder or foot if they can reach. I've never been a star, the athletic or academic
hero. If this is what that feels like, I understand the allure. It feels like the rush
of drugs to me, but I appreciate how healthy this is, this moment of triumph.
I don't know what will happen to all of us, but I'm willing to bet it will be
something better than this.

The doors open and we're outside and there's an ambulance waiting, but
there's also a mob of reporters and onlookers. The reporters call out to me,
and the onlookers ask if I've seen their children. The EMT looks down at me.
"Told you, that livestream went viral."

I prop myself up on one elbow and the cameras flash. The cops block
what they can, but the crowd is practically beyond control. What lies inside
the building behind me is an insane story that's still unfolding. "Kenny!
How'd you do it? How'd you get the video out to the world?" a reporter
screams.

"Michelle," I say, but there's no way he heard me.

The EMT places a hand on my chest. "Easy, Kenny. They'll get the full
story, eventually."

"Kenny!"

I have a momentary lapse, where I feel as if I'm back in the ward, because
that voice, the one that just pierced the crowd, is Michelle's. "Stop!" I yell,
and the bed halts.

"What is it? Are you okay?" the EMT asks.

I ignore the question and scan the crowd. Michelle is working her way
toward the front, to the barricade. "That's her, the one who made the video
possible," I say.

The EMT scans the crowd and seems to be looking where Michelle is battling to get through. "Let me get her," he says.

Michelle has made it to the cops, who will let her go no further.

The EMT talks to the cops, who turn, see me and their eyes widen. He points at Michelle, and I nod. The EMT and the cops exchange a few more words and then hoist Michelle onto the platform.

She runs to me and breaks down at my side. I kiss the top of her head and say, "Thank you."

Michelle manages to speak through her tears. "We did it."

"*You* did it."

She pulls back a bit and examines me. "Are you okay? What she did..."

"I'm fine. She used a scalpel. EMT says the clean cut makes for an easy patch job." I look Michelle in the eyes. "Because of you. I can't thank you—"

She puts a finger to my lips. "Cut that out. You thank me by making this worth it, by staying clean."

Every fiber of me wants to say yes, but I know, I know all too well how much of a lie that would be. "I will do my best, I promise. I need help, though."

"I know you do. That's why you came to me. We all need help, and I'm glad you're finally admitting it. That's like the first step, right?" She smiles.

My heart fills. "It is. This, right here, is the best first step, ever."

Michelle hugs me, gently. "I'm glad you feel that way. But, you're not quite through."

I tilt my head and genuinely have no clue what she means.

"Look at that. You're already in the right position."

"For what?"

"For this." Michelle kisses me, straight on the lips, ever so softly.

I forget to close my eyes, but then do, and the moment transports me out of my life, out of my shattered body, and into a state I've felt so many times before, but never like this, never so naturally.

We separate and the crowd behind Michelle goes insane. "I'd offer you a ride," I say.

She laughs at this. "I'll be fine. You do the same. I'll come to you when they let me."

"Thank you," I say, and do not want to go, but it's time.

Michelle drifts back slightly, ignoring all the calls to her, and I am ushered into the ambulance. I watch her recede as we pull away. The EMT says, "So, that's Michelle?"

"It is."

He pats my shoulder. "Good job. It seems like you both care for each other. That's the ticket."

There's such truth in his words, because I used to be in love with heroin, probably still am, but not in the same way, not anymore. You can't love a drug, because it will never love you back. You can't feel how I feel, now, in a one-sided relationship. Drugs are fun, that will always be true. But only at the start, only as a thrill. Then they become something so much more, none of which is worth it. None of which is worth your life.

26

I awake, stiff and sore, my mouth as dry as sand. My eyes focus, the room comes into view, and so do my parents.

"Kenny?" Mom says. "Kenny, how are you?"

"Water." I reach for a cup. Dad adjusts the straw to my lips.

I drink and then ask, "Prop the bed, please?"

My parents juggle with the bed remote while my vision becomes more clear, as does the pain. The bed moves into position and I ask, "What are they giving me?"

Mom looks at the IV bags. "Just saline. You can't—"

"I know, Mom. I wasn't looking for Morphine. I'm just sore."

"I'll call the nurse," Dad says and hits the button.

They sit and stare and I don't know how to begin this. "I'm sorry," I say.

Mom places a hand on my shoulder. "Not now, honey." I can hear the tremor in her voice. "We don't have to do this now. Take it easy."

I shake my head. This moment with my parents was bound to come, and I should be more prepared, but I'm not. "You need to know this, now. I'm sorry for what I did, for what I've put you through."

"We're sorry for what *you've* been through," Dad says. "Had we known."

"There was no way of knowing," I say.

"But somehow you knew what to do. You went to Michelle. And now?"

"What, now? I don't know."

A nurse appears, scans us, but then comes into the room. "Well, look who's awake. How's our hero feeling?"

I feel the blush in my cheeks, but say, "Sore. Can I have any pain medication?"

The shadow that crosses over the nurse's face is one I've seen a hundred times before. She thinks I'm med seeking. Already. After all of that, and I still want drugs.

I speak before she can. "I don't want drugs. Tylenol. Aspirin. Whatever the doctor ordered. I'm in pain and would like some help."

Every head turns toward me, and even though I'm looking at the nurse's smile, I am sure my parents are doing the same.

"I'm pretty sure it's Tylenol, but let me double-check, and I'll be right back." She squeezes my foot before she goes, and it reminds me of getting wheeled out of the ward.

"What happened to everyone? The patients? Hobson and Williamson? Have you seen Michelle?"

"It's been crazy," Dad says. "The news has been at our house and all over town. The patients have all been reconnected with their families or admitted to hospitals or rehab facilities. Right now, they're talking about how to safely remove what was in all of you. Fortunately, they have Hobson and Williamson in custody, and they're cooperating. As are the rest of the employees. They face Federal prison if they don't, so. Because of what happened, the executive order has been rescinded." He pauses, then his voice breaks and the tears fall. "Jesus, Kenny. I'm so glad you're alive." He bends over me and kisses my forehead, and I can't help my own tears from falling.

Mom wipes her own away. "We saw Michelle and her family and we thanked her as best we could. But it was brief. The police are talking to her, and so are federal agents."

"She's not in trouble, is she?"

"No," Dad says, "I don't think so. But they want to know how she did what she did. So, we haven't had a chance to properly thank her."

I nod and the nurse returns with liquid Tylenol and I feel like a child slurping it down, but I know it's for the best. She checks my vitals and pokes around my wounds, but says that all looks good and I should just rest.

After she leaves, I say what I know needs to be said. "I need to go to a rehab facility."

"Are you feeling like you need to use?" Mom asks.

"No, but I will."

They look at each other and then Dad says, "We've already talked to the facility here. They're taking on patients from the program and have agreed to save a space for you. If you want."

I've been through the center here. It sucks. The rooms are for shit and the food is terrible. The counselors are completely incompetent. Unless they aren't, and I was just in denial of everything.

"Okay," I say. "Let's do that. Who knows, I may end up with some of the guys I know."

They don't want me to see them clasping hands, because they keep them beneath the bed, but I see them, their hope. It's good.

"Are you sure? Wouldn't seeing those patients bring up bad memories for you?" Dad asks.

"Maybe. But that's going to be unavoidable at this point. I may as well just face it head on." I shrug. "Plus, I really like the crew I was with. Even if I could be with one of my ten." I say this and immediately think of Chase and Mike and wonder where they are and how they're doing.

"But that was just a guise, right?" Dad asks. "The one in ten thing, it wasn't real?"

I drink some more water. "It was, though. I know that sounds stupid, but it felt good to be connected. If there's a silver lining, that's it, I guess."

"It doesn't sound stupid, honey. I'm sure your uncle would agree."

Theo and his journal. So much of this started there. I look forward to swapping stories with him, once I'm completely rehabilitated. I think he and I have a lot in common.

My eyes flicker and I feel sleep pulling me under. "Hey, before I fall asleep, I just wanted to say I love you. I don't know when the last time I said that was, and truly meant it. But my head's clear enough, now, to say it and to mean it."

My parents embrace me and we all cry, and beneath their hugs and their tears and their pain and their hope, I fall asleep.

* **

"Look at him. How adorable."

I open my eyes to Chase's voice, sure that I'm dreaming. But he and Mike stand at the end of my bed.

"Holy shit," I say, because I can actually speak now. Two days of rest have done wonders for me.

Chase and Mike rush up to me and then gently hug where I'm not bandaged. "How are you?" Mike asks as he looks me over. "You seem to be doing all right."

"I am. I've been sleeping a lot, but walking, too. I can actually stand upright."

"Unreal. Just unreal," Chase says. "I've watched that footage so many times. You are a friggen warrior."

I don't even need to ask what he means, because the footage is now the video that's been seen around the globe. It's the most popular video ever, and as much as the government has tried to delete it, they've failed. The internet is a slippery playground.

"Forget that. How are you guys? Where have you been?"

They sit and we catch up and they tell me about being in the farmhouse and then one day going into town and seeing what happened on the news. Then they reached out to Chase's family, who took them in on one condition.

"What's the condition?" I ask.

"That we go to rehab together," Chase says.

"Wow. That's fantastic! Where are you going?"

"Same place you are," Michelle says, as she swings through the door.

We all look at each other, totally confused, and then Chase and Mike rush to her and hug her much harder than they hugged me. It's clear this is the first they've seen her, because they ask about what's going on.

Michelle pushes through them, to me. "Hey," she says, and then kisses me. "Sorry, I couldn't get here sooner. There's just been so much."

"Sit, sit," Chase says and he slides a chair out for Michelle. While he does, he and Mike both glare at me, clearly catching the fact that Michelle is here in more than a friend capacity. And they are eating it up.

Michelle sits and tells us about the government coming to her house and about them having her demonstrate how she hacked in, which according to her wasn't that difficult, which pissed the government off, because it's all supposed to be a super confidential and encrypted code. "But I hacked into another system for them that was built the same way."

"No shit?" I say.

"Yeah, they're furious, but told me to get my education and then feel free to submit my resume."

"Don't work for them," Mike says, "make them come begging. Like this guy." He pats my leg.

We all laugh at that, and it hurts like hell but I try not to let them see the pain. "Best decision I ever made," I say.

Chase and Mike pretend to swoon and I shake my head.

"First, though," Michelle says. "I talked to your parents. They cleared you medically, but are you mentally ready for rehab? Like a real one?"

"Hold up!" Mike says. "You said he's going where we're going. How do you know that?"

"Please, if I can hack a government program, I can see who Kenny's going to be in rehab with."

They stand up and cheer. "Hell, yes, the team is back together!"

Michelle frowns. "Is rehab really this exciting?"

"No," I say. "But being with them will make it livable."

"When are you going?" Chase asks.

"I don't know. They haven't told me."

"Let's go, now. That's the other reason we're here. Seeing you is awesome, but we're all set to check in."

I look at Michelle and don't want to go anywhere. I want her with me. But as I realize this, I also understand that I am falling for her, and that's not okay. Not yet. I'll just trade one addiction for another. I take her hand. "Will you bring us down?"

"There's nothing more I'd like to do than take another first step with you."

Mike and Chase swoon again, but I ignore them and page the nurse. When she arrives, I explain what's going on and after a series of phone calls, between my parents and the facility, I am cleared to enter rehab, again.

We all take the elevator and it's a festive moment, which is so strange. But I guess we've been down so far for so long, that there's no other way to go but up.

Yet, when we get to the door, I can't move. I grab Michelle's hand again and squeeze tight. "I don't know how long I'll be inside, but you'll be at school by then, I'm sure."

"Most likely. But you can use a phone here. Call, text, all that."

"You know I will, but I also want you to have fun, make friends, kick the shit out of college. Don't worry about me. You're so damn strong, and I want you to use that strength for yourself."

"I am, and so are you. So, remember me, telling you, that you've got this." She leans in and we kiss, and when we pull apart, she says, "I expect you to reach out as soon as you have privileges."

"I promise."

We kiss again and then Chase and Mike separate us so they can say their goodbyes to Michelle. She waves at us as we enter the ward and I blow her a kiss.

***

It still looks run-down. It still smells like feet. I bet the food is going to suck. But who cares? None of that matters. The people do. The support does, and I'm already armed with more than I've ever had.

We're checked in and given our room assignments. We're all with guys from the program, but none from our ten. It's fine, because we all have a bond because of what happened. We click, immediately, and then we have group.

The counselor is one I've had before: a slim, blonde woman, mid-forties, who looks as if this job is wearing on her. But she smiles at us and says, "So, here we are. With so much in common, but also with such ground to cover." She pauses and looks us over. "Therefore, let me start with a question you can all answer." She points a finger into the air. "What is your takeaway from this experiment you were a part of? What have you learned?"

There's a lot of talk about not trusting the government and a newfound paranoia for how disposable we are, but then the counselor looks at me and I know I have to speak to something deeper.

The room shushes when I clear my throat, and that's something I'm going to have to get used to.

"I used to think that the risk of heroin was always worth the reward, because sometimes, sometimes, that hit was just perfect." There's a collective agreement to this, but I'm not done. "And now, after everything we've been through, I think that risk still applies." The counselor gasps, but I hold up my hand. "Not to drugs, but to life. We have been given a second chance, because regardless of how many facilities you've been in, that last one—the government's—was going to take your life—something we all somehow managed to avoid doing to ourselves. Which, statistically, is pretty damn astounding.

I don't know if this is the facility that will ultimately help you kick. It might be. It might not. But the truth is, you have to give it your all. You have to be willing to try. Second chances are as rare as that perfect hit, and if we were willing to chase that one, we should be willing to chase the other."

I look across the circle, at Chase and Mike, and their eyes are wet. Mine are the same. We've been through something life-changing, together. We have to respect it.

I continue. "I don't know about you all, but that one in ten idea had me. Maybe not all the points and such, but just the fact that I knew nine people were dependent on me, and I was on them. I don't know if that's proper counseling, but it felt good. So, I think we should be there for each other. Don't lose sight of your own issues, but share them. With the collective amount of knowledge we have, I am sure somebody here will have an answer."

The counselor shifts in her seat and I look at her.

"Am I talking too much?"

"No, not at all. Continue."

I look around at the guys, all of these teens, who were cyborgs, who were about to be erased and turned into who knows what. But heroin would have done that, too, eventually. Already had in some cases. It's practically unfathomable, and yet here we are, with so many still out there.

"I guess the one thing about addiction that is the hardest—that secret I don't even reveal to myself—is the isolation. I've got my drugs and no one else. But at the same time, I know that's not true. There are other people trying to help, but I push them away. Or my addict does. He's an asshole."

The group laughs at this. So does the counselor.

"We're not alone, though. Even if you have no one else because you're homeless or your family has kicked you out, or all your friends have died from overdosing, *you're* still here. Technology won't save us. We'll save us. One day at a time."

A hush falls over the room, and then Mike gets up. "Bring it in," he says.

The rest of the patients all stand and we put our hands into a circle, like a team, like Mike and Chase and I did before.

"What's our motto?" Chase asks Mike.

"I wanted to go with *Fuck Heroin*, but Kenny's got me thinking deep."

The group laughs at this and the counselor eyes us nervously, but there's a flicker of excitement as well.

"How about the motto from the ward," one of the kids says.

"I agree, I liked the one in ten. I liked the motto," someone else says.

Everyone nods and agrees with this, so Mike leads us. "Okay, then. On three."

We count off and then yell, "Stay clean by any means."

Our voices dissipate and we take our seats. Previously, that notion felt harsh, and considering how it was being implemented, it was downright heinous. But in our hands, with everyone having each other's back, it's perfect. Because part of staying clean is accepting that it isn't Hell, that life isn't perfect, but that it's never going to be. Just like us. But that doesn't mean we should be given up on, and that definitely means we shouldn't give up on ourselves.

Acknowledgements

I knew this novel would work after I first uttered the premise: *what if the government took over care of heroin addicts?* The look I received told me all I needed to know, that this rabbit hole was one worth pursuing.

It took years for me to get the story correct, to discuss the ways in which addiction and the perversion of power might look in our world, and how a bunch of teens could upend it.

But stories of the outcasts, those on the fringe, those capable of amazing things if only given the opportunity, those are the stories I tell, and this one screams that message.

Too many have been lost in the epidemic of opiates and heroin and fentanyl, and too many more will be victims of whatever is next. Because something else will come along. It always does. We cannot ever give up on the hope that recovery is possible, through any means necessary, just not the ones offered here. I fear the dehumanization of anyone with an addiction, and it is not a stretch to see the government's ability to do just that on a sweeping scale. Look out for one another.

Thank you to all of the people who helped me got back on my feet when I did not think another book was a possibility. You are my light. As always, thank you to Mark Ayotte, my first reader, and the one who always says, "I can't wait to see where this goes." Enormous thanks to the Goat Posse. This literally couldn't have happened without you. Natalie Cammarata, thank you for being my number one fan and for your editing skills. This book is simply better because of you. And a thanks is certainly necessary to Barb Furan for the cover design. What a perfect image to encapsulate this story.

Thank you to my family for being so patient, and for so delicately asking, these past few years, "How's it going?" and for understanding when I didn't have an answer. Well, now I do.

As always, an unimaginable thanks to my wife, Carrie, and to my daughters, Grace and Kaygan, who never gave up, even when others had. My love and adulation to you for everything you have done.

To all the librarians and English teachers and bloggers and book sellers who will get this novel into the hands of teens, thank you for the work you do. The stories that are told matter. They represent who we are and who we can become. Thank you for having faith in my work.

Backlist

If you enjoyed *One in Ten*, then you will also enjoy my previous work:

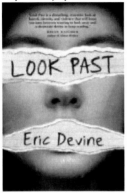

Someone brutally murdered Mary Mathison, daughter of a prominent and very conservative local pastor. Whoever it was is now taunting Avery, a transgender boy, with disturbing messages, claiming that Mary's murder was revenge for her relationship with Avery. The killer's demands are simple and horrific: Avery must repent for changing his gender identity, or he will be the next one killed.

Can Avery deny who he is to catch Mary's killer? Or will sacrificing himself be the ultimate betrayal?

Amazon[1]

When Greg Dunsmore begins filming his weight loss documentary, he never intends to film the hazing rituals of the high school's beloved lacrosse

---

1.   https://www.amazon.com/Look-Past-Eric-Devine/dp/0762459212/ref=sr_1_2?keywords=Eric+Devine&qid=1571995503&s=books&sr=1-2

team. Once he does, he must find somewhere to go with his evidence, before he is discovered and everything is turned against him.

Amazon[2]

Teenage friends participate in increasingly dangerous stunts, which are posted to YouTube, first as a prank and then for money from an unknown financier.

Amazon[3]

2.   https://www.amazon.com/Press-Play-Eric-Devine/dp/0762455128/ref=sr_1_6?keywords=Eric+Devine&qid=1571995745&s=books&sr=1-6

3.   https://www.amazon.com/Dare-Me-Eric-Devine/dp/0762450150/ref=sr_1_4?keywords=Eric+Devine&qid=1571995745&s=books&sr=1-4

With no way out of his life of poverty, abuse, and threat of a meth-dealing biker gang, Tony turns to the MMA gym with his friend, Rob, as an outlet. Will the gym be enough to help Tony find an escape?

Amazon[4]

This is me, thanking you one last time for reading. If you want to reach out, you can find me here:

ericdevine.org   @eric_devine   @ericjohndevine

---

4.   https://www.amazon.com/Tap-Out-Eric-Devine/dp/0762445696/ref=sr_1_3?keywords=Eric+Devine&qid=1571995745&s=books&sr=1-3

Made in United States
North Haven, CT
18 March 2022